The Oregon Trail™

OREGON CITY OR BUST!

by JESSE WILEY

Houghton Mifflin Harcourt
BOSTON   NEW YORK

hmhbooks.com

The text was set in Garamond.
The display text was set in Pixel-Western, Press Start 2P, and Slim Thin Pixelettes.
Illustrations by June Brigman, Yancey Labat, Ron Wagner, Hi-Fi Color Design, and Walden Font Co.

ISBN: 978-0-358-11787-2

Printed in the United States of America
DOC 10 9 8 7 6 5 4 3 2 1
4500770145

The Oregon Trail™

3

THE SEARCH FOR SNAKE RIVER

The Oregon Trail

You are a young pioneer headed West by wagon train in the year 1850. You and your family have already braved nearly half of the perilous frontier path known as the Oregon Trail, crossing 820 miles of territory in what will later become the states of Kansas, Nebraska, and Wyoming.

For fifteen miles a day for more than two months, you have walked beside your oxen and covered wagon. You can't ride in the wagon because it holds everything you need for the journey and for your family's new lives as farmers in Oregon.

You've crossed mountains, prairies, and rivers, and you've passed famous landmarks like Chimney Rock and Devil's Gate. You've also faced wild animals, stampeding buffalo, and learned to start a campfire with dried buffalo dung. You now know how to handle livestock and you've met members of the Cheyenne Nation, among other indigenous people. Best of all, there are still months of adventure ahead of you—*if* you can survive the dangerous ford of the wild Snake River at Three Island Crossing!

⭐ ⭐ ⭐

Only one path will lead you safely through the book to the Snake River, but there are twenty-three possible endings, full of risks and surprises. Along the way, no matter what path you choose, you will experience natural disasters, sickness, and other hazards of the Trail.

You're in a desert without water! What can you do?

A rattlesnake is ready to strike!

A forest fire roars nearby, how will you survive?

Before you begin, make sure to read the *Guide to the Trail* at the back of the book, starting on page 154. It's filled with important information you'll need to make wise choices.

You're not alone, and you'll get advice from friends, Native American people, or Ma and Pa—but sometimes it's best to trust your own good instincts. Make smart decisions and you'll find your way to Three Island Crossing!

Every second counts!
Think fast.
What will you do?

→ **Ready?** ←

BLAZE A TRAIL TO

SNAKE RIVER!

"Roll the wagons!" Caleb, your wagon train captain, commands. It's still early, but you scramble to help get your family's wagon moving with the rest of the train. Even though you've been on the Oregon Trail for over two months now, you're still impressed with how quickly everyone in your wagon train manages to finish morning chores, have breakfast, and repack the wagons before the starting bugle sounds. Then you set off on a full day's hike, which usually covers fifteen miles a day, though you've slowed down a little since entering the pass through the Rocky Mountains.

"When can we stop for lunch?" Samuel asks almost as soon as you start walking alongside your wagon.

You can't help but smile at him, even as you roll your eyes. Your little brother asks the same question every single day—and always just after breakfast.

"As soon as you see the sun touch those trees," Pa replies to Samuel, and points to the distance.

"Are we going to see anything interesting today?" your younger sister Hannah asks, tugging on Pa's sleeve.

You're curious about what landmarks are ahead, too. A week ago, your wagon train left Devil's Gate, a towering chasm cut right through the cliffs and the most remarkable sight of your journey so far. Plus, Caleb surprised you by taking you to a spot where you dug for ice, buried underneath the ground.

"Today we should reach South Pass," Pa says.

"It's the part of the trail where we finally enter into Oregon Territory," you say. "The Land of Promise!"

Ma looks at you with a wide smile. "We'll have finished half of our journey by then," she says.

Halfway at last! Your heart swells with pride that your family has made it this far. Ten weeks ago, you started your travels on the Trail in Independence, Missouri, after leaving your comfortable home in Kentucky in March. But then you sigh deeply as you realize that you still have an equally long way to go.

It's hard to imagine that this wide and gently sloping path is leading you through the Rocky Mountains. Pa tells you how the pass was discovered by fur traders over thirty years ago. Without the path, getting through the mountains would be impossible for the ten wagons that now make up your train.

"Here, boy," your friend Eliza calls out to Archie, your dog. Archie runs up to Eliza with his tail wagging. She hands him a morsel of bacon that she saved for him from breakfast.

Eliza and her brother, Joseph, Caleb's children, have become your best friends. Some of your favorite memories of this trip include the time spent exploring and playing games with them. And Archie has become really attached to Eliza, who takes the time to brush his coat after a long day's hike and always remembers to give him treats.

You walk for a few hours until it's time for "nooning," the midday rest everyone anticipates. Caleb had sent you, Joseph, and Eliza a little ways ahead of the wagons to help scout for a nice spot to rest. Ma likes the midday break because no one has to build a fire or cook anything. Instead, she pulls out leftovers from breakfast as a snack. You happily nibble on some cold flapjacks that were cooked in bacon grease, while the oxen rest and sip from the stream nearby.

"These are the Pacific Springs," Pa says. "We've left home waters behind."

"I'll drink to that," Caleb says, raising his water-skin with a grin. "From this point onward all waters flow into the Pacific Ocean instead of the Atlantic. We have just crossed the Continental Divide."

You take a moment to think about what that means. You've moved from the eastern part of the continent into the West. Amazing!

Hannah and Samuel take a nap in the wagon,

lying on their feather mats. You notice the soles of their sturdy walking shoes are almost completely worn out again after being repaired just a few weeks ago. Yours are in equally bad shape, and the rocky terrain ahead is only going to be rougher.

"We all need to make a very big decision in a couple days," you hear Caleb tell your folks. "We'll be reaching the Parting of the Ways."

You listen closely. With a name like that, you know it has to be important.

"At that point, there are two ways to go," Caleb continues. "We can continue on the Trail, or take the Greenwood Cutoff."

"What is the cutoff?" Ma asks.

"It's a shortcut that will take at least five or six days off our journey," Caleb explains. "But it will take us through a desert."

"How many miles of desert would we have to cross?" you ask.

"About fifty," Caleb explains.

"What's the other option?" Pa asks.

"We'd be heading south, toward Fort Bridger, and would have to cross the Green River," Caleb replies. "I've heard good and bad things about both options, so think about it."

For the next two days, all everyone talks about is the Parting of the Ways. When you finally approach the famous fork in the Trail, it is unmistakable. One set of wagon ruts leads to the left, toward Fort Bridger, while the other leads right, toward the cutoff. In the middle is a wooden pole. Plastered on it are scraps of paper with the names of those who have traveled through already, indicating which road each of them decided to take.

People in your group have strong opinions about which path is better. Some are convinced that saving a week with the cutoff is the only option that makes sense, even if it means crossing a desert. Others are frightened by the idea of a waterless journey and want to stick with the road to Fort Bridger, even if it means crossing the tricky Green River.

Pa turns to you to help decide which way to go. "What do you think we should do?" he asks.

If you say you should head to Fort Bridger, turn to page **126**

If you say you should take the Greenwood Cutoff, turn to page **106**

kay, let's run!" Joseph whispers, pulling you up by the hand. "Once they see us taking off toward our camp, they will probably leave us alone."

You start to move, hoping Joseph is right. The Shoshone people are still several yards away from you.

But suddenly you see Pa and Caleb approaching on horseback. They have found you!

Caleb brandishes his rifle. "Halt!" he shouts. You realize that he thinks you are in danger. But no one has done anything to you!

All the Shoshone people draw their bows and point arrows toward Pa and Caleb. Your heart is pounding as you realize this could start a battle. And Pa and Caleb are outnumbered.

"Hold on!" you shout, jumping in between them.

Joseph raises his arms. "We're okay, we're okay," he says breathlessly.

You see Pa look at you with a mixture of fear, anger, and relief. You feel a rush of guilt realizing how worried he must have been about you.

Caleb dismounts from his horse and walks slowly toward you. He's still holding his weapon, facing the drawn bows and arrows. Pa starts to get off his horse when an arrow zings through the air near his horse's neck.

"Whoa!" Pa cries. The horse startles and then takes off, with one of Pa's legs still in the stirrup.

"Pa!" you shout, as your father starts to get pulled along the ground. Caleb races after the horse on foot, trying to get it to stop. It finally does, but only after Pa has been dragged for several feet.

Caleb and a young Shoshone man help Pa down. You watch nervously as they lay Pa on the ground and carefully examine his injuries. Pa is unconscious and his leg is twisted in a way that it shouldn't be. It makes you want to throw up.

The Shoshone people end up taking all of you back to camp. They send a healer to help set Pa's leg straight and give him some medicine to help him. But it will be several months before Pa can walk again, and he's likely to limp for the rest of his life. In the meantime, he'll have to give up his dream, which has become your dream, too, of getting to Oregon.

☞ THE END

You're so upset about what happened to Gertrude that you agree to accept the gift from the Native American people. The animal skins won't bring your pet back, but they might come in handy for your family along the Trail. Maybe Ma can use them to make moccasins for your family when your shoes wear out completely. Your feet ache in your hard shoes, and the soles have worn thin, even though Pa repairs them with buckskins any chance he gets. The Lakota men bring you the skins, along with a beautiful woven blanket. They hand you the gifts, nod, and quickly leave. They seem kind, and, as they ride away on their horses, you wonder what type of relationship you might have had if you had tried to be friends.

You continue to travel toward Fort Bridger, plodding along as usual. But you start to feel more and more tired. Every day seems harder than the last. The walking for miles each day is almost unbearable.

One day, you try to sit in the wagon instead of walking. "What's the matter?" Pa asks.

"I'm not sure," you reply. "My legs are feeling really tired."

"Okay," Pa says. "Rest up as much as you can."

You know that sitting in the wagon just makes the trip harder on the oxen, but Pa looks at you with concern and lets you stay there longer than usual. That night, when you make camp, you don't feel like eating much.

"You've hardly touched your food," Ma says, examining your plate. "Is something wrong with it?"

"No, it's great," you say, picking at the cornmeal pudding with bits of bacon in it. "I'm just not feeling very hungry."

You see Ma exchange a worried look with Pa. You try to force yourself to take a few more bites, but the pudding won't go down your throat.

Later, as you lie in your tent, your legs ache and you have trouble falling asleep. Ma comes in to check on you while you are tossing and turning on your feather mat. You feel a cool hand on your forehead.

"You don't have a fever," Ma says. "I don't know what is wrong with you."

"I'll be okay, Ma," you say. "I probably just need to sleep."

But the next morning you feel even worse. You trudge along, even though it's hard to catch your breath. When everyone sits down to rest and snack during the midday break, you just rest your head on the side of the wagon. You can't eat anything at all.

Ma and Pa talk about what to do for you.

"I'm going to mix you up a drink of water, sugar,

and salt," Ma says. "That might help bring back some of your energy."

"Or what about a little citric acid mixed with some water and vinegar?" Pa suggests.

You don't feel like eating or drinking anything. But you know you have to take something. What do you ask for?

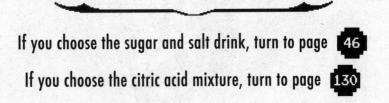

If you choose the sugar and salt drink, turn to page **46**

If you choose the citric acid mixture, turn to page **130**

Everyone agrees that the windlass sounds too risky to try. They want to stick to something more familiar, so they decide to just lead the oxen up the steep hill very slowly.

Pa tries to lighten the wagon for the animals by giving each of you something to carry. You have to haul a sack of coffee beans in a bag across your back.

The rocky hill proves tricky to climb. You watch each of your steps carefully to make sure you don't stumble. Pa leads the oxen up the hill, holding their yokes with a rope.

THUD!

One of the oxen slips on a rock and falls to his knees. The ox sharing his yoke falls, too. But with some coaxing, they get back on their feet and resume inching their way up the hill. When you finally get to the top, Pa takes a look at them and sadly shakes his head.

"I think this one might have a break in his leg," he says. "And the other one's knees look shaky."

"I'll clean them and wrap them up," Ma offers.

"That might help for now," Pa says. "But these animals will need time to heal. We can camp here for a few days and see if some rest is good enough. Or we can go back to Fort Bridger and see if they still have extra oxen for sale. That might save us some time."

What do you do?

If you head back to Fort Bridger, turn to page **51**

If you give the oxen some rest, turn to page **30**

If we try to run, the flames will just keep coming after us," Pa argues. "We won't be able to stop running."

You grab your bedrolls and some food from your wagon, and start leading the oxen up the mountains. Everyone is moving so quickly, it's hard not to stumble and slip on the rocks. You pull Hannah by the hand as you make your way upward. She tries her best to keep up, but at times you have to just yank her and drag her along.

"Faster!" Pa shouts.

As you climb, you feel the fire gaining on you. The air grows thick with smoke and it gets harder to breathe. You feel your legs start to burn with the exertion, and you cough from the smoke.

"Put this over your nose and mouth," Ma says, handing you a damp cloth. You try to breathe through it, and it helps. But as you scramble over a rock, the cloth falls from your hand.

You climb for what seems like forever. But it's working! You look behind you and see the forest ablaze, but you seem to be high enough that the flames won't reach you.

Pa finds a cave and you take shelter in it, huddled together, staring at each other in silence. Everyone is too exhausted and shocked to even speak. Your faces are covered with black soot and all you can make out is each other's eyes. If the situation weren't so scary, you would think it was funny.

Only one ox and your cow have survived the escape. Tears start to roll down your soot-covered face, dripping onto your lap. You are lucky to have survived, but you realize that the rest of your oxen and probably some people from your wagon train have perished in the fire. Your family decides to stay for a few days in the cave while Pa hunts for food. But then you'll have to figure out how to go on without your wagon or any supplies.

 **THE END**

No one is excited by the idea of going back to Fort Bridger. It was bad enough the first time around.

"I can't go back to that horrid place," Ma says.

"I still have nightmares about that rattler," Hannah adds.

Everyone agrees that the trip back isn't worth it, especially since you don't know what kind of animals they will have available for sale. Plus, everything you are forced to buy on the Trail is extremely expensive, so you might not even be able to afford a new set of oxen.

Instead, you make camp at the base of the Big Hill and wait for the animals to heal. The grazing conditions aren't great, but every day Pa scouts for the best place to let them eat and regain their strength.

After a few days, the oxen look better. Ma takes care of their dressing and thinks that the injuries are healing nicely. But the bad news is that while they improve, you are not feeling well at all. You start to have severe stomach pain and after a day or two you have diarrhea. By the time the oxen are ready to go, you are ready to move on, too . . . only not to Oregon Territory. You die of dysentery.

☞ **THE END**

Steamboat Spring sounds more exciting to you, so you head there. Unlike other springs that hiss, this one spits out a stream of water, as tall as you, every fifteen seconds. The water whistles as it shoots up.

Being at the spring feels refreshing. One woman in your wagon train bakes bread with the soda water. It's the fluffiest bread you've had on the Trail. You camp and then trek four days to Fort Hall.

"Welcome," a tall man says as you arrive at the fort, a small stone building popular with fur traders and mountain men. The man, a fur trader named Henry, invites your group to supper. You're glad Ma and Pa accept, because you can smell something cooking that makes your mouth water.

A little while later, you sit at a table and poke at a pinkish steak on your plate. You wonder if it might still need to be cooked.

"What is this?" you whisper to Pa.

Henry just laughs.

"This is the finest of fish: Pacific salmon. Enjoy!"

You bite into the fish, which is unlike anything you've ever tasted. It's delicious! But then Henry says stuff that makes your stomach twist into knots.

"You know the most difficult part of the Trail is ahead of you—the mountains and the Columbia Valley. It's rough, with snow and dangerous rivers. I think it's crazy to take heavy wagons through it."

"Are you suggesting we stay here?" Pa asks.

"You could. But even better, you could go southwest, along the California Trail."

"Why that way?" Ma asks.

"It's easier, with greater rewards. Haven't you heard the stories of all the gold there?" Henry asks.

Pa is silent, but you can see that he is thinking about what Henry said. Ma looks worried and you know she is contemplating the dangers ahead.

Later, a few of the people in your wagon train start to talk about taking the California Trail. They don't want to deal with the harsh conditions on the Oregon Trail anymore, and they're tempted by the idea of gold.

Others want to continue to Oregon and fulfill their long-held dreams of free land promised to each family. They don't trust the fur trappers, who they think just want the territory to themselves. Others have made it, they argue. Why can't you?

It looks as if the train is going to split apart. What does your family decide to do?

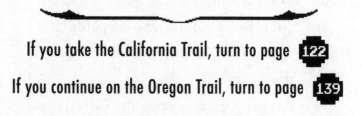

If you take the California Trail, turn to page **122**

If you continue on the Oregon Trail, turn to page **139**

You pick at some of your food. Even though you're grateful for the gesture, you just can't bring yourself to eat any of it. While everyone else seems to enjoy the meal and conversation, you try to ignore the growling in your stomach.

"I noticed you didn't eat anything," Ma says as you walk back to camp. "You must be starving."

"I am," you admit, a little embarrassed.

"I'll make you some beans," Ma says, with an understanding look. "Fetch me some water from the wagon while I start a fire."

You hurry to the wagon, but in your haste, you accidentally grab the container of oily water that Pa uses to clean the wagon wheels when there is mud stuck on them. You hand it to Ma, who pours it into the pot and adds the beans.

You're so hungry you start eating right out of the pot, even though the beans haven't cooked all the way. They taste a little funny, but you eagerly eat them anyway.

Finally, with a full stomach, you go to bed. But you wake up in the middle of the night with stomach cramps. In the morning your cramps are much worse.

The next couple of days are terrible. You have chills and diarrhea. You even vomit! Ma and Pa are so concerned about you that they tell the wagon train to go ahead while they try to nurse you back to health. But soon they have to leave you behind. You die of dysentery.

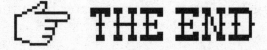 **THE END**

Let's go soak our feet first," you say, and Eliza
leads the way. Archie runs along with you, barking
excitedly. As you walk, a geyser suddenly erupts near
you, and it startles everyone. You all laugh, but Archie
takes off running in the other direction, scared.

"It's okay, boy, it's just water," you shout. But
Archie continues to run farther away. You call for him
a few times, but he doesn't listen to you.

"You guys stay and soak," you tell Joseph and
Eliza. "I'm going to get Archie."

You run toward Archie and call him again.
"Come on, boy, let's go." But now it's turned into
a game. Archie wags his tail. He must want you to
chase him.

"Here I come," you laugh, jumping over a few
of the tiny springs that separate you. You are almost
next to him, when one of the springs shoots off as
you are jumping over it.

YOW! The water is scalding, and it feels like you
are on fire. You fall to the ground in pain, screaming
for help. Your arms and legs are severely burned.

Joseph comes rushing over to you. "What happened?" he says in a panic. And then his eyes grow wide as he sees your burns.

"Get help!" Joseph shouts to Eliza.

You lie there in a tremendous amount of pain. After a few moments you see that Ma, Pa, and Caleb are by your side. Your burns are so severe that they hesitate to move you. Ma gives you some cool water to drink and wraps you in the cleanest cloth she can find.

You won't be able to walk anytime soon. Even worse, you are at risk of terrible infection on the dirty Trail. You had no idea that some of the springs were hot enough to cook a steak. But as the water hisses and steams, your insides burn, and you realize that your dreams of getting to Oregon have just evaporated into thin air.

☞ **THE END**

ait for me," you call out to Joseph, and run after him. You don't want him to snoop around by himself. And if he *does* find the animals, you want to be part of it. You imagine the looks on everyone's faces as you tell them where the missing animals are!

"Thanks for coming with me," Joseph says.

"What if we get caught?" you ask again, feeling your stomach flip over with nervousness.

"We can always say that we are lost," Joseph says. "No one is going to do anything to two kids."

Joseph speaks with confidence, so you try to push

your fear away and scramble to keep up with his long strides.

As you approach the wagon train, you hide behind a big rock so you can observe. There are a bunch of families going about their morning chores and making breakfast. Your stomach growls as you smell eggs frying. *Yum!* Your mouth starts to water.

"Look! They have chickens," you whisper to Joseph.

"Yeah," he mutters, counting their animals. "But it doesn't look like they have what we're looking for."

"What now?" you ask.

"Let's go to the Shoshone settlement."

"Okay," you say, although now you just want to go back to camp and have breakfast. You hope no one has noticed that you're missing yet. Ma gets worried really quickly.

As you approach the settlement, you can see Native American people, dressed in breechcloths and leggings, walking around. Several cooking fires are burning as the community prepares its own morning meal.

Joseph points to a tree. "Let's hide over there, and watch to see where they keep their animals," he says.

Your heart pounds as you get closer. Suddenly, a young boy spots you and starts to stare.

"Duck!" Joseph orders, pointing to a bush. You hide, but moments later a group of men, holding what look like spears, bows, and arrows, heads toward you.

"Look!" You grab on to Joseph's shirt. "What is happening?"

"It's okay," Joseph says. "Just let me do the talking."

"What are you going to say?" you ask, trying not to panic.

"I told you, I'll just tell them that we're lost," Joseph says.

"Let's just make a run for it," you say. "We can still get away."

You see Joseph deciding what to do. Do you stay still or start to run?

If you stay still, turn to page 77

If you run back to camp, turn to page 18

Let's look for higher ground," Ma encourages, while you and your siblings groan.

Pa nods. "I'm sorry we'll have to walk a bit more," he says, "but this way we won't have to worry about the river. It looks like it could flood."

You try to ignore the ache in your feet as you continue walking. Finally you find a spot which satisfies everyone, and at last you all stop.

Ma uses dried buffalo chips, dung that you've collected along the Trail, that she's saved for damp conditions to build your campfire. You help Pa make camp. It's too wet to set up tents, so you'll sleep in the wagon, as crowded as that is with all your stuff in it.

Once you sit down in front of the fire with a plate of hot food, everything seems better. But after you eat, you notice your throat is sore.

"Ma, my throat hurts," you say.

"Mine, too," Samuel adds.

Ma looks at you both and frowns.

"I'll make you some hot tea," she says. "And then you should get to bed early tonight."

The next morning, when you wake up, your throat is a little less sore. But you have a cough instead. Samuel is doing better and is running along the wagon as usual, kicking up dirt. The ground has dried out and the area you are walking through is dusty and bleak. There is nothing but sage bushes, and after a few miles of hiking, poor Archie is covered in what looks like ashes.

"I can hardly see anything but Archie's eyes," Hannah says, pointing at him. "Look!"

Your throat is tickling again so you take a swig from the water-skin and try not to cough from all the dust in the air. But at night, once you've settled on your soft feather bed, you start to cough a lot. After a while, you grow hoarse and your stomach hurts from all the coughing, but you still can't stop.

"Can you stop that, please?" Hannah complains. "I can't sleep! Can't you take some medicine?"

Samuel is snoring, but Hannah is a light sleeper. You try to stifle your coughs, but it doesn't help.

Caleb keeps a medicine chest, including tonics, that help with coughs. Maybe you should take some. Caleb always says yes when anyone asks for medicine, but you don't want to wake him. Maybe you should just go get the medicine yourself. What do you do?

If you take some of the tonic, turn to page **113**

If you just try to sleep without it, turn to page **117**

You slowly sip on water that is mixed with generous amounts of salt and sugar. Even though it makes you gag, it helps you to feel a little stronger. But over the next few days, the pain in your legs gets worse. Your legs tingle and throb all day long and keep you awake at night. Eventually you are so wobbly, it feels like you've forgotten how to walk. Pa spreads out your feather bed and lays you down in the wagon. The bumpy ride mixed with the smell of the oxen makes you feel nauseous, and you have to keep a bucket next to you.

As the days go by you start to feel more and more terrible. Then your gums start to bleed and the next day you are horrified to find your teeth have actually become loose. Only they're not your baby teeth. As you get sicker and sicker, everyone else in your family starts to feel ill, too. Hannah and Samuel cry because their legs hurt, and because they are scared to end up looking and feeling like you. They're right to be scared, because you will eventually die of scurvy.

☞ THE END

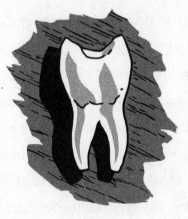

"We'll just make camp here," Ma tells you, much to your relief. It's been a long day of hiking and the last thing you want to do is traipse through more mud to find another spot.

Ma tries to light the few buffalo chips she's saved for an emergency, but it's too damp to get a fire started. So instead you eat a cold supper of buffalo jerky and prairie biscuits, then go to bed. Even though there's food in your stomach, you're not fully satisfied. You fall asleep imagining a sizzling steak with mashed potatoes and green beans, complete with a nice slice of chocolate cake for dessert.

BOOM! CRASH!

"What's that?" Hannah's wide eyes peer at you from under her blanket. You've all been startled awake by a violent thunderstorm.

"It's just thunder," you say, trying to sound brave. Archie whimpers and nestles his body against yours. "Everything will be okay. Try to go back to sleep."

But it's impossible for any of you to fall asleep as long as the storm lasts. Each time the thunder claps, you jump, and the sound of the wind howling is worse than coyotes. The rain pours down with such force that it bends the tent. Finally, after what seems like hours, the rain starts to slow down. You drift back to sleep.

You wake to a different scary sound: shouting, from outside your tent. You poke your head outside and gaze in horror at what you see. Half the camp seems to have vanished, including heavy stuff like boxes of dishes and the animals' yokes. Some of the wagons are filled with water, their contents floating under the canopies.

"What happened?" you ask Ma. "Is this just from the thunderstorm?"

"It looks like flash floods," she replies grimly. "It was a mistake to camp here. We should have known that the water level was too high, and the ground was too wet."

"The storm just did us in," Pa adds, shaking his head. "It would have been safer to keep moving to higher ground to camp."

Your family didn't lose as much as everyone else, but you've lost enough to keep you from going farther. Entire sacks of flour have been torn open and filled with water. Without your food supply, the risks of starving on the Trail are too great to continue. In a flash, your dreams of Oregon are over.

☞ **THE END**

You are going to try to make it back to Fort Bridger to get more oxen. Pa suggests that Ma stay camped with Hannah and Samuel at Big Hill while the two of you hike to Fort Bridger. It's nice to have some time alone with Pa. Along the way, he tells you stories of his childhood in Kentucky.

When you arrive at Fort Bridger, traders approach you with an offer to sell you oxen.

"That's four times what I paid back in Missouri!" Pa cries. "I don't have that kind of money."

"I'll tell you what," one man says. "I can give you these two mules for the price of one ox."

Pa looks unsatisfied but knows he doesn't have many options. He hands over the money and you head back to Big Hill. The mules are a little difficult to guide along the way, but Pa thinks they just have to get used to their new owners. He suggests tying the animals to a tree and making camp. You loosen the ropes that have been holding the mule you've been leading.

OW!

Once it's free, the mule kicks you in the stomach and runs off, back toward Fort Bridger. You fall to the ground, clutching your gut. Pa gets kicked, too, except in the leg.

"I think it's broken!" Pa says, unable to stand.

You help Pa as he limps back to the rest of your family. Unfortunately, you'll have to return to Fort Bridger while Pa gets medical help. You hate the fort and the idea of being there any longer, but for now it's where your dreams end. Be sure to keep an eye out for snakes!

 **THE END**

You decide to head to the lake by yourself, planning to surprise everyone with the filled water-skins. Then in the morning, you can take everyone back to see the lake for themselves and refill your water barrels for the rest of the journey through the desert. You imagine Ma's face lit up with her biggest smile, the one that means she is bursting with happiness. And you wonder if maybe Caleb will agree to let everyone go for a quick swim before you have to head back on the hot dusty Trail. You always feel so dirty on the road, and on this stretch you've felt extra sweaty and grimy.

As you walk toward the lake, you can't wait to dip your hands into the crystal clear water and wash them clean. Then you'll drink the cool water to your heart's content. You know it will be the most refreshing and delicious water you've ever tasted.

You walk a little faster, admiring how the rays of the sun are reflecting on the water. The water sparkles and shimmers and is the deepest color of turquoise. But it's still so far away. As you stumble over a rock,

you notice that you don't seem to be getting any closer, even though you've been walking for a long time now. The lake must be farther away than it seemed. You decide that it must be hard to estimate distance with nothing but sand around you.

You start to run toward the lake. You're panting heavily and your legs are tired, but you can't stop now. But no matter how hard you run, the lake only seems to get farther away. Your head is hurting now, and you start to feel dizzy. For a moment it looks as if there are two lakes instead of one. You stop and blink hard.

You wonder why you're feeling so strange. *What's happening to me?*

Soon your legs buckle and you fall to the ground. You can't move another muscle and your head is pounding. You have severe heat exhaustion. The lake is only a mirage. You think you see something that's not really there. But what *is* real is the fact that you've been wandering in the hot desert for a while and no one knows where you are. Your chances of being found are extremely low.

 **THE END**

The snake is looking you straight in the face. Its head keeps swaying from side to side as its pointy tongue flickers. It feels like you have been lying there for hours, but only a few moments have passed. You try to move your arm slowly to the side, but you see the snake's head follow your motion, as if it can anticipate your next move.

You're so terrified that you just can't take it anymore. You jump up from the floor. "Snake!" you scream at the top of your lungs.

Before you get very far, you feel an intense pain as fangs pierce the skin on your leg. As quickly as the snake has struck you, it slithers away. You fall to the ground. Everyone else wakes up from your howling.

"What happened?" Pa asks.

A warm tingle travels through your body. You can barely speak.

"S-s-s-nakebite," you finally say, and point to your leg.

"What kind? Where did it go?" Pa says, with panic in his voice.

"It was a rattler," you manage to whisper.

Your eyes start to roll back in your head, and the last thing you see is Pa's stricken face as he cradles you in his arms.

☞ **THE END**

Getting off the Trail is too scary to consider, you decide. Who knows what you might find? It's safer to stick to the road others have traveled before you.

You continue along the path, but before it gets any better, it gets worse. The conditions become harsher. You enter into an area that is nothing but desert.

"I'm so hot," Samuel complains. He takes off his hat and mops his face, which is red and sunburnt.

You don't even have the energy to reply, so you just concentrate on moving one foot in front of the next. Your legs feel like lead and all you want to do is sit down with a cold glass of lemonade.

"I'm thirsty," Hannah whines.

Ma and Pa are saving most of the water you have left for the family. The oxen are struggling to keep moving, and you're afraid that they will eventually collapse and die. You've seen piles of animal bones along the Trail, bleached by the hot sun.

As it gets harder to keep moving, your wagon train starts to travel by night instead of day, to avoid the intense sun. It feels weird and a bit spooky to move in the dark, led by the light of a couple of lanterns, and you are forced to move slowly to avoid stumbling. But your oxen team continues to get weaker. The animals are moving slower and slower every day.

After a night's hike, everyone is too hot and tired to even consider building a fire. You eat a cold supper of jerky, cold beans, and cornbread. And your family talks about what to do moving forward.

"I'm afraid that we can't continue like this without the oxen dying on us," Pa says. "If we don't get them some grass or water soon, we'll be stranded."

"But we don't know when we'll find those things," Ma points out.

"That's true," Pa continues. "So that leaves us with a hard choice."

A feeling of dread settles over you.

"We can unload as much as possible from our wagons to make the load lighter for the oxen,"

Pa says. "That means
dumping everything that
isn't essential."

"What's the other
option?" Ma asks.

"We can abandon the
wagon and carry as much
as we can on our backs. A wagon might not be able to
cross the mountains that are up ahead anyway. This
way, we load up the oxen with some supplies, but it
will be easier for them than pulling the wagon."

Everyone in your family falls quiet as you think
about what makes the most sense. What do you decide?

If you unload your wagon, turn to page 95

If you abandon the wagon, turn to page 90

You decide that traveling by night will be too dangerous, since it will be hard to see where you are going. Plus you would hate to run into bandits or coyotes roaming the desert. Instead, you form a wide line, leaving plenty of space between each wagon, and start to move forward that way. It helps some, and you find that you cough less with fewer dust clouds in the air.

But even with this adjustment, you're still drinking too much of the water you've brought. At this pace, you will run out really soon. Everyone starts to cut down on the amount of water the animals get, to save more for the people, but that just makes the oxen weaker. You see them struggling.

"We need to find a water source, quickly," Caleb says, "before the animals start to die."

"But we can't! That will mean going off the Trail," Ma protests.

"And we don't know where or when we will find anything," another man says. "We could just end up wandering around longer in the desert heat."

"What if we send out a search party for water while the rest of the group rests and stays camped?" someone suggests.

"That could be dangerous," Pa says. "We should stick together."

"We have to do something," Caleb says. "What will it be?"

If you send out a search party, turn to page **74**

If you stick together, turn to page **92**

You reluctantly break off a little piece of the root cake and nibble on it. Not bad! Pa was right. It does taste a lot like a sweet potato. You hungrily eat a big piece.

"How is the stew?" you ask Joseph. He is licking his fingers, satisfied.

"It's really good," he says with a big grin.

You take a small bite and realize he's right. In the end, you have a pretty tasty meal, although you stay away from the bear root bread.

After everyone has eaten, your hosts serve you some berries and nuts for dessert along with a fragrant hot tea. Then a young man, wearing beaded moccasins and leather pants with fringe on the sides, gets up and everyone hushes.

A moment later, someone starts to bang on a drum while others chant and the man starts to dance in a way that you have never seen. His body bends and he stomps gracefully in a pattern, making circles on the ground. His hair is long and sleek and he is holding a feathered bow. It looks like he is using his body to tell a story of hunting, and the drumming and chanting gets louder and softer as he moves faster and slower.

When the dancer is done, another gets up and tells a different story. You can't take your eyes off of the performers, each one more graceful than the last. Everyone else is completely fascinated, too. And so the night continues until Samuel starts to nod off and Ma motions that it is time to head back to camp.

★ ★ ★

The next morning, it's time to part with Roaring Cloud, Bright Sky, and the rest of the people you have met. You feel a lump in your throat as Roaring Cloud looks you in the eye and nods slowly.

"Goodbye," you say, wondering if you'll ever see him again. Hannah runs to give him a hug. Roaring Cloud looks surprised at first, but then you see him hold her tight for a few seconds.

You spend the day traveling to Fort Bridger. Everyone is looking forward to getting there in order to replenish much-needed supplies and make repairs to their wagons. Plus, it's been awhile since you were at a place with buildings and traders. But when you arrive at the well-known Fort Bridger, it's not what you expect at all.

"That's it?" Eliza grumbles. "Those hardly look like log cabins!"

You can't believe your eyes, either. Fort Bridger is a collection of a few rickety wooden buildings belonging to the fur trappers who live here with their

Native American wives. They don't have much to
trade—mostly furs, skins, moccasins, and blankets.

Ma is the most disappointed of all; she was
hoping to send letters back home and buy some more
molasses. But at least there is a blacksmith shop, where
Pa gladly gets shoes for the oxen and replaces your
cow.

That night, when you're sleeping in one of the
wooden huts instead of your tent, Archie curls up by
your feet as usual. But then, suddenly, he growls.

"Shush, Archie," you say, and start to roll over.
But then you freeze. On your feather mat, staring
right at you, is a big rattlesnake! You hear the rattling
sound, and it makes your heart stop. Do you jump
up and run away from the snake as fast as you can, or
lie still and hope that it leaves you alone?

If you run away, turn to page 56

If you lie still, turn to page 143

You're too afraid of the quick-moving current to let go of the rope you're holding on to, even though you're a good swimmer. Instead, you scream as loudly as you can. "Somebody, grab that wheel!"

You see a man from your wagon train try to reach for it, but he misses. Joseph then attempts to catch the wheel with a rope, but he isn't successful, either. The wheel continues to float down the river, and your heart sinks as you watch it disappear out of sight.

"Pa!" you shout again, breathlessly. "We lost our wagon wheel!"

Pa turns around to see what is happening. As he checks to make sure everything else in the wagon is secure, one of your oxen loses his footing on the soft sand of the river bottom. The ox stumbles and falls over, pulling down the animal attached to him. Soon the two oxen are tangled in their yokes, and are suddenly swept underwater.

"Get up!" Pa yells, as he desperately tries to pull them up onto their feet. But they are just too big and difficult to handle. You try to help, but the oxen are thrashing so wildly you're afraid one kick from their powerful legs will knock you out.

Finally Pa gives up. "We have to keep moving," he shouts, with a grim expression. Slowly you make it to the first island.

Your family assesses the damages. The two oxen have drowned, and your wheel is gone. You may be able to get to the other side of the river, but after that, your wagon isn't going anywhere. Many other families in the wagon train have also lost animals, items from their wagons, and in one case, an entire wagon that flipped over.

Everyone huddles on the island, afraid to cross the next part of the river and dreading what's ahead. Even if you make it back to solid land, you'll have to make some hard choices about what to do next. Getting to Oregon City seems impossible now.

 **THE END**

You walk over to where your father is talking to a group of men.

"Excuse me, Pa?" you say, hesitant to interrupt.

"What is it?" Pa asks.

"I have something to tell you," you continue, motioning that you want him to step aside with you.

Pa walks away from the Shoshone to listen to you privately. You tell him about Joseph's plan to spy on the other camp and the Indian settlement to look for the missing animals. He looks at you with concern.

"That is a terrible idea!" he says. "He could get lost, or be accused of stealing himself. It's a good thing you told me."

Pa rushes over to Caleb and tells him what happened. They team up with another two men and head out to track down Joseph.

"Where did he go first?" Caleb asks.

"To the other camp we passed, I think," you say, not wanting to meet Caleb's eye. What if he blames you for letting Joseph go?

You wait anxiously with Ma, pacing until everyone returns. Finally, after what seems like hours, you see them walking back. *Phew!* Joseph is with them and you breathe a big sigh of relief.

Joseph walks right by without even looking at you. You know he's really upset. But Pa tells you that the other wagon train didn't have your animals, and they were actually in really bad shape themselves.

"They said they had been through enough and were ready to go back," he explains. "They weren't interested in anything other than the fastest route home."

"Then what about the stolen animals?" Ma asks.

"We just have to forget about them," Pa says. "Anyone could have taken them. We may never find them and we don't have time to waste trying to track them down."

"We'll just have to be extra careful from now on,"

Caleb adds. He pats you on the shoulder, giving you a look that means that everything will be okay.

Over the next couple days, every time you try to talk to Joseph, he turns away and ignores you. But finally, he starts to speak to you again.

"I guess it was a bad idea for me to go off like that," he says. "And you were only looking out for me." You just nod, and the matter is over. You're back to being friends. It's too lonely on the Trail to let small arguments ruin a friendship.

The next day, you arrive at the infamous Green River Crossing. The river is known to be difficult to cross, especially in the spring, when the winter snows melt and raise the water levels, creating strong currents. This time of year, in July, the water is a little lower, but you still have to walk across the river on narrow gravel bars. Another option is to use the ferry that some mountain men have created, but they charge a fee.

When you arrive at the crossing, the area around it has been transformed into a big camping site. You see lots of other travelers, and rut marks of other wagons that have come before you. As you make camp, Caleb goes to find out how much the ferry will cost you.

A bit later he returns, slowly shaking his head with disappointment.

"The ferry is being repaired," he says. "It will take at least four days to get it running again."

Four days! That is a long time to wait and it will delay you. There is a line of wagons already ahead of you. At the same time, the ferry might be the safer option, even if it is the more expensive one. Everyone debates the two choices: crossing the river yourselves or waiting for the ferry. What do you decide?

If you wait for the ferry, turn to page **100**

If you cross the river, turn to page **133**

Caleb organizes a small group of men to leave with him to search for water.

"How much water do you have left?" Caleb asks.

"If we ration what we have, we should be okay for about three days," Pa replies.

As the search party leaves, everyone is silent.

"I think it's a mistake for us to split up," Ma says firmly.

"I agree, but I hope they come back with water soon," Pa replies.

Everyone's patience is running low from being thirsty and overheated, so you organize a game for Samuel, Hannah, Eliza, and Joseph. You climb under your wagon where it's shady and take turns making shadow puppets and guessing what the shapes are. For a few moments everyone forgets how hot it is.

After two more days, you are running drastically low on water. Pa says that if the search party does not return soon you will have to move ahead without them and look for water yourselves. You look at

Eliza's and Joseph's sad faces and imagine how worried they must be about their father.

The next day, when there is still no sign of the search party, Pa says you must leave.

"Don't worry about Caleb," he says to Eliza and Joseph to reassure them. "I'm sure he will find us."

You get back on the Trail, but within a few hours one of your oxen collapses. One by one, each wagon starts to lose animals.

Two more of your oxen lie down, and you tug on their yoke to encourage them to get back up. You feel a warm wind kicking up behind you, sending little pieces of sand flying and getting in your eyes. Within minutes you are caught in the midst of a fierce sandstorm. The powerful wind and swirling hot sand pelt you relentlessly. There's no place to hide, and even though you cover your nose and mouth with your shirt, sand still gets through. You fall to your knees, try to protect your face, and wait for the storm to pass.

When the sandstorm dies down, you cough up bits of sand and begin to search for your family. You discover Hannah crying because another pair of oxen have died. Your family is stranded without any water, any animals to pull your wagon, and, soon, any hopes of survival.

 **THE END**

Help!" Joseph says, coming out of the bush with his hands raised.

You stand behind him as the Native men approach you.

"We lost a cow and a horse," Joseph continues. "Can you help us?"

"We haven't seen your animals," says the youngest of the men.

"Someone stole them last night," you say.

The young man speaks to an older man wearing a rabbit fur robe. Then he turns back to you.

"There is a tribe known for stealing animals. What they do is wrong. We will get your animals back," the man says. "Where is your wagon train?"

Joseph tells them and looks at you with a big smile. You head back to camp, excited to tell the others the good news.

"Where have you been?" Pa says, furious, when he sees you. "We've been looking everywhere for you!"

"But Pa," you start to say.

"I can't believe you would disappear like that, without telling anyone where you went," Pa continues. "Your mother is worried sick."

You feel terrible, and hope that Joseph is having a better time breaking the news to his dad. But later Joseph comes around looking glum.

"Pa didn't want to hear anything about what we found out," he says. "He was so angry!"

But a little while later you see the Shoshone people you encountered earlier walking up to your camp. And they have your missing animals!

Your wagon train welcomes them and invites them to a feast. Everyone cooks up the best meal possible, with one wagon member breaking out tins of fruit saved from the beginning of your travels on the Trail. And you send the people of the Shoshone Nation back to their settlement laden with gifts.

That gives Pa a big idea.

"I'm sorry I got so upset at you," he says. "I think your meeting these people is one of the best things that has happened to us in a while."

Pa explains that he wants to start a business with the local people, offering services to other pioneers. "We can help people who have lost animals, want guides, or need food and water," Pa says. "And I'm sure people will want to trade and buy things from us, which will make us a good living!"

Your family's dreams of getting to Oregon aren't gone forever, just on hold for a little while.

☞ **THE END**

Eliza," you call out softly, tapping her on the shoulder as she sleeps in the shade of her wagon.

"What time is it?" she asks, still groggy. "Do we have to start walking again already?"

"Not yet. It's still the afternoon," you say. "But I have to show you something incredible."

Eliza sits up now, looking curious. "What is it?"

"I found a lake!" you say. "Will you go with me to get some water? We can surprise everyone when they wake up."

Eliza gives you a puzzled look.

"A lake?" she asks. "That's impossible. We're in the middle of a desert."

"No, look! It's right over there." You point toward the shimmering water.

Eliza looks at you with concern now. She tells you that you're just seeing a mirage, which is something that isn't really there, and gives you a few sips of water to drink. Then she wakes up Ma and Pa.

Ma touches your skin gently. "You're burning up!" she says.

You start to feel a little nauseous and lie down, and soon you pass out. You have heat stroke and are breathing rapidly. Everyone is trying to get your body temperature down any way they can. But there isn't much they can do without cold water or ice.

Luckily you *do* wake up, but you are much too weak to continue on this journey. And pretty soon, without any water, the rest of your family is feeling the same as you. You never imagined that something as simple—but as precious—as water would end up destroying your dreams of Oregon.

☞ THE END

I t's decided," Caleb says, after everyone agrees. "We'll float the wagons across the river."

A couple days later, you reach the infamous crossing of the Snake River. You make camp early along the banks of the river, and spend the rest of the day preparing for what's ahead. Next comes the big task of unloading the wagons and taking them apart. Everyone helps. Once your wagon is empty, Pa gets to work removing the axles and the wheels. That leaves him with the box of the wagon, which he caulks and seals carefully with wax to make it as waterproof as possible.

Caleb suggests keeping the animals yoked, so they'll be easier to lead through the water, even though they won't be pulling the wagons. When

everything is ready, you walk to the banks of the river and gaze out over the wide expanse you'll have to cross. The water rushes by swiftly, and the current is a little frightening. It makes you gulp.

"We'll hold on tight to the animals or to the wagon as we cross," Ma says, seeing your face. "It'll be okay."

Ma isn't as strong a swimmer as you, so you know she must be nervous. You smile and nod as reassuringly as you can. But inside, you're still a little scared, too.

The next morning, you form a line and make your way into the water. You're heading for the first island. The cold water comes up to your waist and you grab on tight to the ropes, leading the oxen, feeling safer as the oxen move slowly but steadily through the water.

"Hold 'em steady," Pa says, looking behind him to make sure everyone is following.

You look behind you, too, and suddenly you see one of your wagon wheels slip out of the wagon. It starts to float away! It will get swept into the current and disappear downstream. But you could still reach it—it's only a few feet away from you.

You pause for a second, deciding whether you should swim after it and grab it. Wagon wheels are difficult to replace on the Trail, and you don't have any more spares. Or you could just stay where you are and hope that someone else grabs it. What do you do?

If you swim after the wagon wheel, turn to page 98

If you stay where you are, turn to page 67

After a vote, it is decided that you're going to build the windlass. This way you have less chance of injuring the animals or damaging your wagons on the steep climb. Even though it will take some time and effort, everyone decides that it's worth trying.

Caleb volunteers his wagon to be used for the windlass. The first step is to empty it out and push it up the hill. Then Pa puts his carpentry skills to work, using ropes and wheels to make a pulley at the

top of the hill. Soon you have an impressive device connected to trees at the bottom of the hill.

You watch nervously as the first wagon makes the trip up Big Hill. It works! The animals are led up slowly next, taking lots of breaks along the way. And finally, after several hours, all of the wagons safely make it up the hill. Joseph is so proud that his idea worked. And you're impressed by Pa's handy skills.

Everyone takes a break at the top of the hill, eating leftover breakfast as a midday snack. Next comes the tricky task of making it down the steep slope. You remember how difficult it was to get down a sharp incline at Alcove Spring, back in the second week of your journey. You used ropes to tie your wagon wheels and make brakes, and it took the strength of all the men to slowly bring the wagons down the hill. This hill is even steeper.

Since it would be so easy to lose control of the wagons, you take all of the same precautions. Then the men hold on to the wagons with ropes and lead them down the hill in a zigzag pattern instead of straight down. A few items fall out of the wagons, but you manage to get down safely.

The rest of the hills you have to surmount are nothing compared to Big Hill, so it's smooth going for the next few days.

One afternoon, Samuel runs up to you. "Guess what's coming up next?" he asks.

"What?" you reply, hoping it's something good.

"Soda Springs!" he says, a note of wonder in his voice. "Pa says the water tastes like it comes from a real soda fountain." You can't remember the last time you drank soda water, but it sure sounds refreshing right now.

"Ma says we can add sugar to the fizzy water for a special treat," Hannah adds with a big smile.

You know right away when you've reached Soda Springs. Everyone marvels at the bizarre landscape, which is unlike anything you've ever seen before. You stare at cone-shaped geysers as tall as Pa, spewing water like miniature volcanoes. There are craters of all sizes and waterfalls, too. But most fascinating of all are the springs, some of which make gurgling and hissing sounds and have steam rising above them.

After everyone finds a spot to camp, you all grab your cups and follow Caleb to one of the soda springs. He is the first to dip his cup in and take a big sip.

"It smells a little funny, but it sure tastes great," he says, grinning.

As promised, Ma has allowed you to add some sugar to your cup. You carefully taste the sweet fizzy water, enjoying the way it tickles your tongue. You're amazed that it came right out of the ground like that!

After you drink your fill, Ma and Pa say that you can explore this wondrous area a little bit with Eliza and Joseph.

"Just be careful," Ma says.

"Let's go," Joseph says. "Can you hear that?"

You hear a high-pitched whistle that reminds you of the steamboats you saw in Missouri.

Joseph points in the direction the sound is coming from. "That's coming from a place called Steamboat Spring. Let's go there!"

"Wait!" Eliza says, "I'd rather go to the hot springs and soak my feet."

Both options sound fun to you. Which do you agree to do?

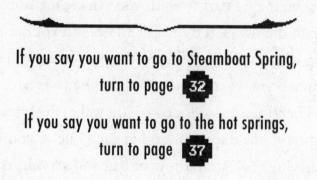

If you say you want to go to Steamboat Spring, turn to page 32

If you say you want to go to the hot springs, turn to page 37

Pa decides that the smartest thing to do is to abandon the wagon and continue on foot. You see the fear on your family's faces at the thought, but Pa explains that it is your best chance of survival.

You've had a long night of hiking, so Pa suggests you get as much sleep as possible.

"Everyone will have to carry supplies from here on," he says.

As your eyes start to shut, you can see the sun rising in the sky. You try to fall asleep, but your mind is racing with the image of the white, sun-bleached bones of animals you have passed. Will that be your fate, too?

When the sun goes down, Ma wakes everyone up. Pa has laid out the supplies that each one of you will be carrying. You strap on your bag and set out, trying to ignore the weight on your shoulders. You overhear Ma and Pa talking.

"How much food and water do you think we have?" Ma asks.

"If we are careful, we can probably make it for

five days, but after that we have to find some water," Pa responds.

★ ★ ★

You have been walking for four days now.

"I think we should stop walking for tonight," Pa eventually says.

You drop your bag to the ground, and you see Samuel reach for the water-skin.

"Let me have some when you're done," you say.

He takes a small sip, walks over to you, and hands you the pouch. You put it to your mouth and just a few drops come out. It's the same with the rest of the water-skins. They are all empty.

You search desperately for water. But there is nothing. Your family cannot survive. As you lie down for the night, parched and weak, you wonder who will pass by *your* bones.

 **THE END**

I'm so glad that we stuck together," Ma says.

"The idea of splitting up didn't sit well with me, either," Pa responds.

Caleb holds a quick meeting about the water shortage situation.

"We have to be extra careful from here on out," he says. "We are dangerously low on water and I don't want anyone to get dehydrated."

You know that Pa has been drinking the least amount of water in your family. He has been trying to make sure that Samuel and Hannah have more. Your brother and sister each passed out once already in the last few days, and Ma keeps staring at their faces to make sure they are not overheating again.

"Pa, do you see that?" You point into the distance, where some riders are on horseback. The dust the horses are kicking up creates a cloud.

Soon they have caught up to your wagon.

"How are you doing today?" one of the men asks.

"It sure is hot out here," another adds.

"Which way you folks headed?" a third man chimes in.

Caleb exchanges glances with Pa and a few others in the wagon train.

"We have some water if you folks are interested," the last man says.

Samuel is quick to respond. "We sure do need some water, mister," he says.

The man reaches into a pouch on the horse and pulls out a container of water.

"It's going to be fifteen dollars a cup," he says.

"That's robbery!" Pa exclaims.

Pa and the men begin arguing and you start to get scared when the strangers shout angrily, right before they ride away. One of them reaches into his back pocket, pulls out a gun, and shoots.

BANG! BANG!

You can hear the gunshots ringing in your ears for some time. And then when they stop, you see that a bullet has ricocheted off of a large rock and hit Caleb in the leg! Luckily the bullet went through his leg cleanly, but it will still take several weeks for your wagon captain to heal.

While you're waiting, Pa discovers a freshwater spring with clear and delicious water. As you camp there, Ma and Pa start to sell fresh pies, quilts, and other goods to thirsty travelers who stop to rest. By the time Caleb is ready to move on, your family is settled, happy, and convinced that this is a better life than the one on the Trail. You watch the rest of the wagon train roll away, as you help yourself to a big piece of pie.

☞ THE END

You decide to unload the wagon as much as possible to make it easier on the oxen. But that means that you are down to the bare essentials for the rest of your journey. You are sad to see the pile of stuff that you are forced to leave behind, from most of your dishes and your only pair of nice clothes, to all of the supplies Pa brought with you for the farm. All you're left with is your bedrolls, camping supplies, work clothes, and most important of all, food.

The idea works. Your oxen team manages to pull the lighter wagon out of the desert and into the Sierra Nevada mountain range. It's beautiful and scenic and a welcome change, even if the Trail takes you over a rocky and at times steep path. It's nice to see trees, and making camp is easier with plenty of wood for the fire.

Things are going well until one day you see a pair of rabbits dash toward you and keep running past

your wagon train. Before you can tell anyone, several mule deer appear from the woods, running at full speed in the same direction as the rabbits.

"Look, Pa!" you shout, pointing to the backs of the deer as they disappear out of sight. "Where are these animals running to?"

As you speak, some big-horned sheep come tearing out of the trees. Birds flee into the air.

"I think the bigger question is, What are these animals running *away from?*" Pa says.

Ma points above the trees. "There's smoke over there!" You look to the right and see a low cloud of dark smoke.

"It must be a forest fire!" Pa says, with urgency in his voice. "We have to get out of here before it reaches us."

You feel fear gripping your heart. "What should we do?" you ask.

"Let's run!" Ma says. "Leave everything behind and follow those animals!"

"Wait," Pa says. "We could try to outrun the fire.

But we could also try to climb high enough into the mountains to be out of harm's way."

"What about the animals?" Ma asks.

"We can try to take them with us," Pa says.

"What about our things?" you ask.

"Just grab what you can carry easily," Ma says. "Whether we run or climb, we can't take too much."

You don't have long to decide what to do. The smoke is heading your way, and you can smell burning now. What do you choose?

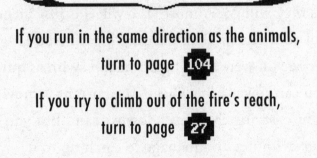

If you run in the same direction as the animals, turn to page 104

If you try to climb out of the fire's reach, turn to page 27

You lunge for the wheel, stretching your arms out as far as they will go. Almost! The wheel is just inches out of your reach. Taking a deep breath, you let go of the rope you were holding on to and swim as quickly as you can toward the wheel. The current is moving rapidly, carrying the wheel downstream. But you are a strong swimmer and manage to catch up to it.

Got it! You wrap your fingers around the wheel, and pull it close to you. It's still floating and starts to carry you like a raft.

"Pa!" you shout, realizing that no one saw you swim away and that they won't know where you are.

You see Pa moving the oxen along, and try to wave to get his attention. But your family and wagon are only getting smaller as you move farther and farther away.

Desperate, you use all your strength to swim in their direction. Your muscles start to burn, but you can't make any progress against the powerful current. It continues to pull you away from where you want to be. Suddenly, you see some rocks in front of you. You manage to steer the wheel and yourself away from them just in time.

BAM! The next rocks are too big to avoid. You crash into them, and right before you are knocked out forever, you wonder if the wagon wheel will still make it to shore.

 **THE END**

Almost everyone agrees to wait for the ferry to be repaired. Even though it will take a few days, you've heard too many stories of pioneers slipping and falling off the gravel path into the swift current of the Green River. Many wagons were lost this way, and both dreams and lives were destroyed.

Luckily the banks of the Green River make for a nice, grassy place to camp where the animals can graze. Pa and Caleb volunteer to help repair the ferry, which gets it operating a day sooner.

When it's finally your time to ride across, you sit in the wagon, which is taken over the rushing water on a wooden planked raft. You hold your little brother's and sister's hands tightly until you are safely across to the other side.

It takes almost a full day for all of the wagons in your train to get across the river. While you're waiting, you, Joseph, and Eliza organize the kids into a game of hide-and-seek.

"You're it!" Samuel shouts and runs away.

You close your eyes and count to fifty.

"Ready or not, here I come," you announce, and look around. No one is in sight except for Archie, who barks and runs toward a bunch of bushes. You follow him to see what he finds.

When you get to the bushes, you hear Archie start to growl softly.

"It's okay, Archie," you say, expecting to see your little brother or sister curled up there. But instead, you gasp. Lying in the brush next to a little pond is a baby antelope! It stares at you with wide round eyes.

"Aw, poor thing," you say. "Why are you all alone?"

You guess the antelope has been orphaned or abandoned, so you go ask Ma if you can give it a little bit of milk in a cup.

"You shouldn't touch wild animals!" she says, following you to the spot. But when she sees the baby animal, she softens and agrees to give you some milk.

The antelope follows you and becomes your new pet. You name her Gertrude and tie a ribbon around her neck. When the wagon train moves, she travels with you, just like Archie.

One afternoon, after you've stopped for your midday break, a bunch of dogs appear out of nowhere and start chasing Gertrude. A moment later, two Lakota men on horses race after the dogs. You run after them, waving your arms and yelling.

"Stop! She's mine!"

A little while later, the Lakota men return with Gertrude tied to the back of a horse, lying limp.

"No!" you cry, realizing the dogs must have caught up to her.

One of the men gets off his horse and speaks to Pa. After the conversation, Pa approaches you.

"The men are sorry their dogs killed your antelope," he says. "They are offering us some deerskins in return."

It's nice of the Lakota people to want to give you something in return for what happened to Gertrude.

But part of you feels like you shouldn't accept it. Their dogs didn't know Gertrude was your pet. What do you say?

If you say that you'll take the gift, turn to page **21**

If you decline the gift, turn to page **108**

Let's run," Ma says. "I'm afraid we won't be able to climb quickly enough, and the animals won't make it up the steep incline."

You grab a few essentials from the wagon and start to run. You hold Samuel by the hand, and Pa puts Hannah on his shoulders. Ma is carrying water and some of your bedding. She tries to keep up, leading the cow behind her.

"We have to move faster!" Pa shouts, as more wild animals run past you. Your oxen have already been unyoked, and they, too, are running in the direction of the other animals.

You hear the breaking of branches and roaring of the flames, and the smoke gets thicker and harder to breathe through. You start to cough desperately, but keep running as quickly as you can.

"You're going too fast," Samuel says. "I'm going to fall!"

"Keep up," you snap at him, yanking his arm. You feel bad for being harsh, but you know there is no other option. Sam has to keep running, even though his legs must be aching as badly as yours.

You feel the heat of the fire grow more intense. It gets harder and harder to keep moving, and more and more difficult to breathe.

"Sam!" you shout as your little brother stumbles and falls to the ground. He lies there, unmoving.

"Sam! Get up!" You shake him hard and roll him over, and see a big gash on his head.

Pa runs back and grabs Sam, handing Hannah off to Ma. You start to run again and for a moment everything seems quiet. You think you might have gotten away from the fire, and wonder if maybe it turned in a different direction. But you're wrong. Within moments the fire catches up to all of you and you are engulfed in flames.

☞ **THE END**

The group decides the cutoff is the better way to go. Not only will you save a week of travel, you won't have to ford the Green River. Everyone tries to prepare for the challenges of the desert ahead. Your water-skins are fully loaded, and you've brought along extra barrels of water.

"It's important to think twice before drinking water," Caleb warns everyone. "We have to make our supply last until we get to another source."

You try to follow orders, but by the second day, it's really hard. The desert is drier and hotter than anyone expected, and it is making you extra thirsty. Plus you can't stop coughing. As the oxen plod along, they kick up so much dust it creates a big brown cloud, making it hard to breathe.

"We can't continue like this," Pa says. "We need to make it easier to travel somehow."

Caleb agrees. "We could travel by night and then rest during the day. The hot sun will be less of a problem that way. Or we could line up our wagons side to side instead of in a line," he suggests.

"What is the advantage of that?" Ma asks.

"That way you won't walk through the dust of the wagons in front of you," he says.

What do you do?

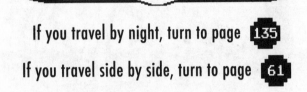

If you travel by night, turn to page **135**

If you travel side by side, turn to page **61**

Pa, the dogs didn't know that Gertie wasn't just a regular antelope," you say. "I would feel bad taking anything from them."

"I agree with you," Pa says, looking at you proudly. "I'll tell them what you said."

Pa goes back to the men and speaks to them. They nod their heads, then jump up on their horses and ride away. But just after you start to hike again, they return.

"We will travel with you as far as the next village," they say. One of the men smiles warmly at you. You learn that his name is Roaring Cloud and his son is Bright Sky. They are part of the Lakota Nation.

The next day, the men accompany your wagon train. Along the way, they point out various plants and tell you what is edible and what they use for making medicines. Ma listens carefully and makes notes in her journal.

Everyone is grateful to have the company of people so familiar with the land. It makes you feel safer. When you make camp, the Lakota disappear, and you wonder if they have left to go back to their homes. But then they come back, just as quickly as they left, and hand Ma a jackrabbit to add to supper. Ma prepares it into a savory stew that everyone shares. And as you sit around the campfire after a satisfying meal, Roaring Cloud tells you stories of his family and Lakota legends.

"Once upon a time, when the world was young, Porcupine had no quills," he starts.

"Really?" Hannah asks, her eyes huge as she listens intently.

"Porcupines were smooth like mice," Roaring Cloud continues, explaining how Porcupine, an animal who lived long ago, discovered prickly thorns from a bush. Porcupine put them on like a coat, then curled himself into a ball to keep Bear and Wolf away.

"Wow," Samuel says, enjoying the story as much as you are. You notice how your new friend's dark eyes shine in the light of the fire and wish that he and Bright Sky would stay with you all the way until Oregon.

The next day you arrive at the Lakota settlement, and your wagon train makes camp nearby. Roaring Cloud invites you to supper for a feast. You, Hannah, and Samuel gather a bunch of wildflowers to take with you. Pa brings some fuel that he's collected for the fire, too.

"This is so exciting!" Hannah

says, smoothing her apron over her dress. Even though it feels like a celebration, you don't have anything fancy to wear. You're still in the dusty dirty clothes you wear on the Trail. You all help Ma wash the clothes by the rivers as often as you can, but it's a process that takes hours. And your clothes get dirty again so quickly anyway.

The settlement is bustling with people coming in and out of the teepees. But one area is set up for the feast. Roaring Cloud greets you with a warm smile and offers you a seat in front of a mat that is covered with plates of food. A woman dressed in elaborate skins smiles at you, and you wonder if she is his wife.

"What's that?" Samuel asks, wrinkling his nose at the sight of the food.

"I don't know," you reply. "But it doesn't look like anything we've ever eaten before."

There is a loaf of bear root bread and wild onion stew and a cake-like thing made out of another kind of root. Pa has eaten the cake in the past, and says it tastes like a sweet potato. But you're not sure about any of this food.

You feel Roaring Cloud looking at you, and wonder if he notices that you aren't eating. You don't want to hurt his feelings, but you are not used to this kind of food. Do you force yourself to eat it? Or do you wait until you get back to your camp and have something safe and familiar, like the leftover beans from last night's supper?

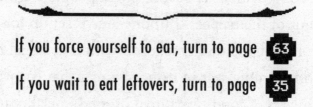

If you force yourself to eat, turn to page **63**

If you wait to eat leftovers, turn to page **35**

You don't want to wake Caleb so you rummage through the medicine chest for the tonic. It's too dark to search for a spoon, so you take a few gulps straight from the bottle. Then you get back to your tent and lie down again.

After a little tossing and turning you finally fall asleep. Soon you are in a heavy slumber and have weird dreams. In one dream, you have taken too much medicine and ended up poisoning yourself. Or is that your fate?

 **THE END**

I think we should get off the Trail," you whisper to Pa.

"I think you're right," he replies. "If we don't find some food for the oxen soon, they won't make it much longer."

Luckily, everyone else finally agrees with you. You're feeling hopeful that conditions are going to get better as you veer south off the Trail. But after you travel for several miles, the terrain hasn't changed much, and you start to worry about whether or not you'll really find more grass or water on this path.

The wagon train stops for the midday break. Everyone starts snacking, but you can't stand not knowing what's ahead.

"Pa, I'm going to climb up that rock to see what's nearby," you say.

"Okay, but hurry," Pa says. "We have to get moving again soon."

You scramble to the top of the rock, which gives you a better view. A deep sense of disappointment washes over you as you stand at the top. As far as you can see, there is nothing but barren land.

Pa looks up at you and motions that it's time to leave. You slide down the rock and hurry back to your wagon. You shake your head at Pa without saying a word. He nods sadly, understanding.

Five days later, the oxen are weak and frail and you have not had a warm meal in days. It's just too difficult to find fuel for fires. You set up camp for the evening, and Ma tries to lift everyone's spirits by spreading the little bit of the molasses she has left on prairie biscuits, as a treat. You lick the sticky sweetness off your fingers, and are feeling a bit better when suddenly you hear the sound of hooves approaching. Is it Native American people, or maybe someone else who can help you? You've heard of groups of people who have made a business of helping weary pioneers.

"Do you think they are bringing us supplies?" you ask Pa.

"I'm not sure," Pa responds with a concerned look.

In the end, the riders don't bring you anything but trouble. They are bandits looking for lost and helpless victims like you. They rob you of everything valuable, including what's left of your money.

After they ride away, you hear nothing but stifled sobs. Now you are left with even less than you had before, stranded in a harsh and unwelcoming land. As your oxen start to die, you realize that you won't ever make it to Oregon.

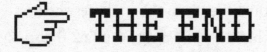 **THE END**

You scrap the idea of rummaging through the medicine chest without anyone to tell you what to take. But soon you see Ma peeking through your tent to check on you.

"How long have you been coughing like that?" she asks, concerned.

You shrug weakly. Ma returns a few minutes later with some medicine and an extra blanket.

"Here, take this and wrap yourself in this blanket," she says.

You drink the bitter tonic. And soon, under the weight of the blanket, you fall into a deep sleep.

Your wagon train is making its way along the Snake River. You've recovered from your cough and are feeling much better. That's a relief, because sometimes coughs are the start of deadly illnesses. Suddenly you hear the loud rushing of water.

"Those must be the Shoshone Falls," Caleb says,

listening carefully. "I've read they're supposed to be very impressive."

"Can we go see them?" Eliza asks. She's always on the lookout for an adventure.

"We can, if everyone doesn't mind extra hiking."

"I hear the falls are one of the wonders of the Trail," Ma says. "I'd like to see them."

Everyone else is equally eager so you agree to make the trek. When you reach the falls, they are one of the most beautiful sights you have ever seen. The rushing sheets of water drop down, foaming and frothing, from the cliffs above. The force of the water is so loud it can be heard from miles away.

A couple days later you come upon another amazing sight along the river. It's an area between two rapids where dozens of Shoshone people are spearing massive fish. You recognize the pinkish fish as the kind you tried for the first time at Fort Hall.

"Pa, look! It's salmon!" you say. "Can we get some?"

"Let's ask," Pa says, looking hungrily at the fish. You've had nothing but bacon and cornmeal pudding for days, and you could all use a change.

Pa barters for several large fish, which he grills over the campfire that night. Ma pulls out some potatoes that she has saved for a long time, and you all enjoy a delicious and satisfying supper.

The feast brings out the celebratory mood in everyone. After everyone is done eating, fiddles and harmonicas fill the air with song. You, Eliza, and Joseph play a game of cards. Samuel and Hannah entertain themselves by stringing together colorful beads that Ma got from the Shoshone people.

The evening gives everyone a nice break, which is important because of the big challenge ahead. You are about to approach Three Island Crossing, which is the hardest part of the Snake River to cross.

"Even though it's difficult, we need to cross the river here to avoid a rough desert route that would take us through massive sand dunes," Caleb explains.

"What is the crossing like?" Pa asks.

"First we have to ford one section of the river, which is about a hundred yards wide, to an island," Caleb says. "Then we cross a swift and dangerous branch to another island, and then there's one more part of the river to get across."

Everyone starts to talk about the best way to get across the river.

"I've heard we should tie the wagons together," one man suggests. "The extra weight makes it less likely that the wagons will tip over or drift downstream."

"Yes, but that is a lot of weight for the oxen," another man argues. "It might be better to take apart the wagons and float them across the river. That way the animals only have to manage themselves."

A discussion ensues about how to float the wagons and whether or not that is a better idea than connecting them together.

"It's up to you all," Caleb decides. "Whatever everyone agrees to do, we'll do."

A lively debate erupts until you come to your decision. What do you do?

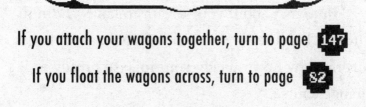

If you attach your wagons together, turn to page **147**

If you float the wagons across, turn to page **82**

The California Trail sounds like a better choice," Pa says to your family privately.

"I'm glad you think so," Ma says. "It also sounds safer to me."

"But what about your dream to have a farm in Oregon Territory?" you can't help but ask. You're surprised by how quickly your folks are ready to change course.

"If California doesn't work out the way we hope, we can still make the trip up the coast," Pa says. "And if there is as much gold as we are hearing about, we'll have all the money we need."

You guess he's right. Why not try out California first, especially if it's an easier trail?

But not everyone else agrees with you. More than half of your wagon train, including Caleb and his family, plans to continue on to Oregon. Three other wagons are joining you, splitting off from the rest. But you'll join up with another wagon train that is heading southwest from Fort Hall, too. That way, you'll have a larger group of fifteen wagons.

You don't think about how hard it will be to say goodbye to Joseph and Eliza until you reach the Raft River Crossing. There it finally hits you. They've been with you on the Trail since the very beginning, and have been wonderful friends. You hold back tears as you say goodbye, but Eliza sobs and holds you tight. Joseph blinks hard and gives you a half hug. When the Trail forks, you keep walking in the other direction.

"It looks like there are some nice people in this wagon train," Ma says, putting her arm around you. She's also sad to be leaving friends behind. You nod, trying to lift the heaviness off your heart.

The trail to California starts off pretty well. For several days you make good time, traveling at least twelve miles a day. But once you pass the Humboldt River, things quickly change. The land grows increasingly desolate and difficult to cross. There is almost no grass, the water tastes bad, and there's very little fuel. But your new wagon train captain, a rough man named Edward, is determined to push ahead.

"It has to get better," he insists.

"What are we going to do?" one man complains. "The animals are getting weaker and we are running out of feed."

"And I can't manage to get a decent campfire going," a woman adds. "We haven't had a proper hot meal for two days."

Everyone is tired, hungry, and frustrated. Soon the discussion turns into a shouting match. Some people agree with Edward, saying that you have no choice but to continue on the trail and wait for conditions to improve.

"If we change course now, it could get even worse," they argue.

Others are convinced that you need to veer off the trail to search for better grass and fuel.

"If it doesn't get better soon, we won't be able to continue," they say.

Ma gets everyone to calm down and talk to each other. What do you agree to do?

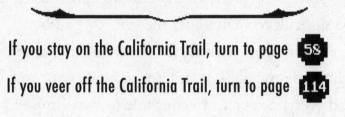

If you stay on the California Trail, turn to page **58**

If you veer off the California Trail, turn to page **114**

Heading south to Fort Bridger seems like the safest option. Your family tells the group you think they should take this route, even though it will take a bit longer. Everyone agrees.

You're relieved. The cutoff would have taken you through the desert. That evening, when the wagons stop for the night, your parents tell you stories they've heard about the desert.

"Some say the oxen drop from thirst," Pa says. "Some families lose their entire teams!"

"And people have to travel at night because it is too difficult to walk under the sun," Ma adds.

You imagine walking the dusty hot trail at night, using only the light of lanterns to guide you. You're glad everyone agreed to continue to Fort Bridger. Forts are welcome spots along the Trail for making wagon repairs, trading goods, and resting. And you especially like meeting kids from other wagon trains.

While your family sets up camp, you walk with Joseph to collect sagebrush for your campfire. Grass is scarce in this area, known as Little Sandy Crossing, and there isn't much fuel.

"Do you ever miss school?" Joseph asks you as you hike together.

"Sometimes," you reply, surprised at yourself. When you first learned you were going on the Trail, you were excited that you wouldn't have to go to school. Now you like it when Pa gives you lessons in geography or grammar and Ma quizzes you in sums and organizes the kids into spelling bees.

"Do you?" you ask Joseph.

"I do, a lot," Joseph says, as you expect. Joseph seems to know a little bit about almost everything.

"I miss books the most," he adds with a sigh. "I've read every book we have at least three times!"

As you head back with armfuls of brush, you point to smoke from another wagon train's camp. Like yours, they have grouped their wagons into a circle, or "corral." This keeps animals safe from wolves, coyotes, thieves, and from wandering away.

"Looks like we have even more company," Joseph

says, pointing to wisps of smoke in another direction. "That's a Native American settlement. The Shoshone are in these parts."

The fuel you bring back is enough to get a decent-size fire going, which Ma uses to cook your supper. You eat baked beans, with a little bit of bacon for seasoning, and some pan bread. At bedtime, you pull out your worn copy of *Gulliver's Travels*. But before you've read three pages, you're nodding off.

You wake up to a guard shouting an alarm.

"We've been robbed!" you hear. "A cow and two horses are missing!"

Thieves! Someone managed to sneak past your guard and steal the animals. It's barely light outside, and you realize it's very early in the morning.

Joseph beckons you over to his campsite.

"One of those groups we saw last night must have robbed us," he whispers. "I'm going to go spy on them. Cover for me if anyone asks."

Joseph takes off before you can protest.

After Joseph leaves, you wonder if you should tell Ma and Pa where he went, or go after him yourself. You don't want him to get angry with you for being a tattletale. But you don't want him to be out there alone, either. What do you do?

If you tell Pa what Joseph is doing, turn to page 70

If you go after Joseph, turn to page 39

Here you go, drink this," Pa says, adding a few drops of citric acid into your water-skin.

"What will that do?" you ask.

"I'm afraid you have scurvy," Pa says, with a worried frown. "We haven't had enough fruit or vegetables in our diet."

You've heard of scurvy before. It's a pretty serious ailment and it can even kill people. Thinking back on all the bacon, beans, and cornbread you've been eating, you're not surprised. You can't even remember the last time you had some fresh fruit. It must have been the wild berries someone collected weeks ago.

Even though you don't feel like eating or drinking anything, you force yourself to sip the water. Slowly, you start to feel a little better, and over the next few days your strength returns. But once you're feeling better, Hannah and Samuel start complaining of the same symptoms you had.

Pa orders everyone to drink the citric acid mix, but you've run out.

"I don't know what to do," Ma says. "If only we had brought along more of that veggie cake!"

You think back to the brown brick-like cake that the shopkeeper had showed you all the way back in Missouri, at the start of the Trail. It was made out of dried vegetables that were pressed into a giant block. At the time, you and Samuel wrinkled your noses at it because it looked like something animals would eat. But every now and then over the first month of your journey, Ma had broken off a piece and mixed it into the beans or rice she cooked.

"We don't have much of a choice," Pa says. "We have to push on to Fort Bridger. Let's just hope they have supplies of citric acid or fresh lemons there. We'll have to pick up what we can and get our strength back. Keep your eyes open for berries."

The fort is still several days away. You hope

everyone can make it that far. Hannah and Samuel are already having trouble walking. Looking at their weak faces, you are really scared and doubtful. You never wished for the veggies you used to leave on your plate more than right now.

☞ **THE END**

You decide to cross the river and look at the water current and the tiny gravel path that lies ahead. The sound of the water rushing makes it hard to hear. Ma holds on to Hannah's hand and you keep a tight grip on Samuel's as you walk behind the wagon. Every so often you can feel the uneven ground beneath you give way a little bit, but you manage to take another step forward.

"We're halfway across," Pa shouts.

You lean your body to the side so you can see Pa, when suddenly your foot slips off the narrow path. You hear Ma scream as Samuel tumbles down with you, into the water. You let go of his hand and try to grab on to something, to keep from being swept away. But the undercurrent pulls you down. You feel yourself flailing, and you swallow huge gulps of water as you desperately try to regain your footing.

Just when you think it's hopeless, a hand grabs you and pulls you up.

"Can you breathe?" Joseph asks.

You nod yes. You start coughing as you get to your feet. You see Samuel is safe with Pa. Joseph guides you slowly along the rest of the path, and you make it across the river. Ma and Pa rush toward you and give you and Joseph big hugs. They're certain Joseph saved your life.

Over the next couple of days, you keep coughing. After a while, the coughing becomes uncontrollable and you can't catch your breath. Soon you're wheezing heavily and have to lie down in the wagon. It hurts to cough, as if someone is squeezing your lungs. It becomes difficult to breathe. You have water in your lungs and will die of pneumonia.

☞ **THE END**

You decide to travel by night through the hot dusty desert. That way the sun won't be beating down on you, making it more difficult to travel. Plus you've already used up more of your water supply than you should have at this point. It's been extremely hard on the oxen to have to pull the weight of the wagons, including the heavy barrels of water, in the blistering heat. Moving under the cover of darkness will be easier on them.

But once you all agree to the plan, you realize that traveling by night means that you won't be sleeping tonight. After a short evening rest and supper, you are going to start moving again and continue until tomorrow morning.

"What if I can't walk another step?" Hannah asks, worried by the idea.

"We can take turns resting in the wagon, so it isn't too hard on the oxen," Ma replies.

Sitting in the creaky wagon with all your stuff isn't very comfortable, especially when it rolls over bumps. But it beats hours of endless walking.

When it gets dark, you head back out on the Trail. You, Joseph, and Eliza hold lanterns to guide the way. It feels spooky to be moving in the darkness by the glow of the moon and the flickering lights.

"Look," Joseph says, pointing to the sky. It's so clear you can see the constellations. You try to identify the ones you know.

"There's the Big Dipper," you say. As soon as the words are out of your mouth, you imagine a ladle being lowered into a big pot of cold refreshing water. But it isn't anywhere near time for a water break, so

you push the thought out of your mind and look for other shapes in the sky.

After a couple of hours of walking, you've lost all interest in the stars and the adventure of moving by night. You want to curl up in your tent and sleep. Your legs are sore and you stumble. Your lips are so dry and parched, you can't help but keep licking them, even though that just makes them worse.

Finally it's your turn to rest in the wagon, but it seems like only a minute before you're walking again. You barely notice the sunrise, and can only think that you are more ready for sleep than you have ever been.

Later you go to sleep in your tent, but you wake up after a couple of hours. It's too hot to sleep. You're sweating. Everyone else is fast asleep, but you walk outside to see if you can catch a breeze.

Outside, you see something glimmering in the distance, reflecting in the daylight. It's a lake! You give a little shout and start to run toward it, before you realize that you should grab the water-skins and fill

them up. Do you take the water-skins and fill them
up yourself so you can surprise everyone when they
wake up? Or do you wake up Eliza so she can help
you carry more water back? She is always game for an
adventure and you know she would be as excited as
you. But you feel bad waking her. What do you do?

If you go alone to the lake, turn to page **53**

If you wake up Eliza, turn to page **80**

Everyone in your family agrees you must continue on the Oregon Trail. It's been Pa's dream for far too long to give it up, and now it's become all of yours, too. Even though the idea of gold sounds tempting, you've heard troubling stories of pioneers being disappointed and tricked by people leading them off the Trail.

Caleb's family is staying on the path to Oregon, which is a huge relief. Not only would it be hard to manage without Caleb as captain, but you also can't imagine the Trail without Joseph and Eliza. In the end, only three wagons decide to split off from the train. You'll be sorry to see them go.

After leaving Fort Hall, you hike for three days through sage-filled plains to the Raft River, which is a deep and rapid stream leading to the Snake River. It's also where the families leaving for California will finally turn southwest. The hike is pretty straightforward, except that it starts to rain hard on the second day and doesn't stop until the third. You trudge through the mud, soaking wet and cold.

When you get to the Raft River crossing, you and the other families who have stayed with the wagon train ford the stream easily. But soon after you get to the other side, you are startled when Joseph nudges you and nods toward the right.

There lies a gravestone that reads: "To the Memory of Lydia Edmonson, who died Aug. 16, 1847, Aged 25 years."

Your heartbeat quickens and a feeling of dread settles over you. So many pioneers don't get the choice of whether to go to Oregon or California.

"What are you looking at?" Hannah asks.

"Oh, nothing at all. We saw a funny bird," you reply, pointing in the other direction. "Look, did it fly over there?"

You feel guilty for fibbing, but you don't want your little sister to get scared. You think she might understand what graves are, but you don't ever talk about them in front of her, even on the bad days when you pass several. Luckily, Hannah is soon happily pointing out all the birds she sees and asking you if they are like the one you saw.

That evening your wagon train searches for a spot to make camp near the Snake River, which is rushing and hitting the rocks along the banks. Its water levels are higher than usual because of all the rain that's fallen over the past two days. Your scout picks out a spot, but the ground is muddy and soaked, and some of the others start to complain.

"This isn't a good spot to camp," one man says.

"It's too wet. Let's go find some higher ground," says another.

But looking for another spot means more walking and you, like many others, are tired.

"This is good enough," a woman argues. "I don't want to walk another step."

"Yes, it's fine. It's going to be wet everywhere," someone else agrees.

Ma and Pa look around at the area, uncertain. Then they look at you kids and see how tired you are.

"Do you want to make camp here, or keep looking for something better?" Ma asks you.

If you say you want to make camp here,
turn to page **48**

If you say you want to keep looking for something
better, turn to page **43**

You remember that a snake rattles its tail as a warning that it might strike. Even though your instincts tell you to spring off your mat and run away, you force yourself to lie still. You hold your breath, slowly counting the seconds in your head.

Archie doesn't move, either, although he looks poised to pounce on the snake. You desperately hope he doesn't.

After what feels like hours, but is probably only a few seconds, the brown spotted snake slithers into a small hole on the other side of the wooden hut.

"WOOF!" Archie runs after it and starts to bark at the hole, as if he is challenging the snake.

"Come here, boy," you say, in a shaky voice.

"What's going on?" Samuel asks in a whisper, his voice heavy with sleep.

"A snake," you say.

"Snake!" Hannah screams, waking up Ma and Pa. Everyone crowds around you as you tell them about your close encounter.

"Good thing you didn't try to strike it or run," Pa says. "Those snakes are deadly."

No one gets much more sleep that night, especially you. You keep checking to see if anything is coming near you. When the morning bugle sounds, you're still exhausted, even though you're not sorry at all to leave Fort Bridger.

★ ★ ★

You've entered Bear Lake Valley, a beautiful area with rolling hills and cedar groves. It's filled with plenty of firewood and water.

But Caleb has warned you all about the next obstacle ahead: the Big Hill. It's one of the steepest climbs on the Trail. After five days of hiking, you finally reach the point where you have to trek up the massive hill. Everyone stares at it in disbelief.

"Even if we get up that thing, how are we going to get down the other side?" Pa asks.

"One thing at a time," Caleb says. "We can do it if we're careful."

"I think we should use a windlass to get the wagons up," Joseph suggests.

"What's that?" you ask. You've never heard of one of those before.

"You anchor one wagon at the top of the hill, and attach ropes to its wheels," he says, getting excited by the possibility.

"Then what happens?"

"You attach the other end of the ropes to the rest of the wagons at the bottom of the hill. Then you turn the wheel on the windlass like a crank. It pulls the wagons up the hill."

"I've heard of windlasses being used successfully on the Trail," another man agrees. "We should try it."

If you use the windlass, the oxen would just have to get themselves up the hill, without carrying the weight of the wagons. But some of the others aren't so sure that it's a good idea. They're nervous about using something they aren't familiar with for the first time.

"What if it breaks?" someone says. "Or if it isn't strong enough?"

They think going slow and steady up the hill might be the best option, even if it would be challenging for the animals.

What do you decide?

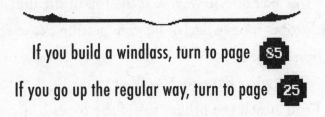

If you build a windlass, turn to page **85**

If you go up the regular way, turn to page **25**

You decide to tie two wagons together and cross the river in pairs. With double the weight, the wagons should be less likely to tip over in the strong current. Besides, the idea of disassembling your wagons and floating the parts across the river sounds like too much work. And there's too much potential for accidents or losing things in the process.

Your wagon is connected to Caleb's with heavy ropes. Soon everyone is ready to go.

"Let's roll the wagons," Caleb orders. "Move them slow and steady. And don't stop in the riverbed, just in case there is quicksand."

The first pair of wagons rolls into the water, and then the second follows. Yours are next. Ma is riding in your wagon with Hannah and Samuel because she isn't a very good swimmer and the water is too rough for her to walk in. You help Pa and Caleb lead the animals, along with Joseph and Eliza.

You step into the brisk water, which reaches up to your waist, ready for the first part of the crossing. You shiver and your teeth start to chatter. Archie jumps in after you and paddles happily.

"You have that thick warm coat, Archie," you grumble enviously.

The other animals are reluctant to get into the water, and you don't blame them. You wonder if it's because they don't want to be cold or because of how strong the current is.

"*Hiyaa!*" Pa calls, pulling them by their yokes. "Come on."

Finally, the oxen take the plunge. Slowly they make their way across the river as you lead them with ropes. Things are going smoothly until suddenly the wagons jerk violently.

SPLASH!

Something has fallen out of one of the wagons.

"Ma!" Hannah screams.

You see your mother's bonnet bobbing in the current, but you don't see the rest of her anywhere. Where is she?

Pa throws you his ropes. "Hold them steady!" he shouts. And then he dives after Ma.

You remember Caleb's warning about stopping in the river, so you keep your oxen moving. But you feel a lump in your throat and you want to cry out for Ma. What if she drowns?

Finally you see Pa swimming back, dragging Ma along behind him. She isn't moving, and he lifts her into the wagon. Then he jumps in and starts to press on her chest and blow into her mouth. As Pa keeps going, your heart pounds so hard it feels like it is going to rip out of your chest. It seems like time freezes until you finally hear a little cough and cry out with relief.

"She's alive!"

Pa gently sits Ma up. She has a cut on her head

that is bleeding and she looks confused, but other than that, she seems okay. Ma hit a rock when she fell out of the wagon. It knocked her unconscious, and she would have drowned if Pa hadn't acted so quickly.

"Can you handle the oxen?" Pa asks, as he dresses Ma's wound.

"Yes," you say, glad that there's something you can do to help.

"Let's keep moving," Caleb says, his face filled with emotion. "That was a close one."

You reach the island safely and take a rest before continuing on to the next crossing. Looking at the second island, you shudder, realizing that you will have to do this all over again.

Pa takes the ropes again and leads the oxen during the second stretch of the crossing. He looks at you from time to time and gives you an encouraging nod. You expertly steer the oxen with Caleb, and before too long, you make it to the other side of the river.

"We did it together," Pa says, smiling at you proudly. You smile back at Pa, and look at the rest of

your family, realizing how grateful you are for every one of them.

You've overcome so many obstacles on this journey so far, and each time you feel even closer to the people who survived them with you. Three Island Crossing is behind you now. Since you left Devil's Gate, you've had plenty of adventures and challenges, from rattlesnakes to the Big Hill. You've had good times with friends like Eliza and Joseph and made new friends like Roaring Cloud. You've tasted foods like Pacific salmon and even drank soda water from the ground!

It's been almost half a year since you left your

home in Kentucky and headed to Missouri to start the journey out West. Your old life seems like a distant memory, and all you know now is life on the Trail, with all its hardships and joys. But you are almost three-quarters of the way to Oregon City.

In the weeks ahead you will have to cross rugged mountains. Luckily your family has made good time since you started out on the Trail in May, so you won't still be trekking in the heart of winter. Even so, you know that the next part of the Trail will be the most difficult. But you're not worried. You've gotten this far, and you're ready for whatever is next. Because you are a tried-and-true pioneer!

👉 **THE END**

Three Island Pass

AUGUST 24, 1850

GUIDE
to the Trail

GET READY TO EXPLORE!

You have completed half of the Oregon Trail, pioneer! You've relied on your wits, good judgment, and resources like this travel guide to get this far. Making it through the rest of the journey requires you to stay alert and to watch out for dangers, from wild animals and harsh climates to swindlers looking to profit off of you. The next part of the Trail also involves difficult decisions on how best to navigate, so be careful and choose wisely.

DANGERS!

FLASH FLOODS

Floods can wipe out entire camps, if you aren't careful to make camp in the right spot. Avoid sites next to rivers with overflowing banks and damp ground.

SNAKEBITE

Snakebites are common on the Trail and can be deadly if the snake is venomous. If you encounter a rattlesnake, do not make sudden movements or strike it. If it rattles, it is scared. Stay as still as possible and it will probably leave you alone.

DISEASE

Staying healthy on the Trail can be difficult. Eat the cleanest and freshest foods you can in order to avoid dysentery. If you get diarrhea, drink water mixed with salt and sugar. Another serious condition is scurvy, which is the result of not eating enough fruit and vegetables. Symptoms include weakness, paralysis, bleeding gums, and loss of teeth. The condition can be reversed by eating citrus fruits or citric acid.

HEAT

If you find yourself in desert-like conditions on the Trail, it is safest to travel by night. Stock up on water and ration it carefully. Watch out for signs of heat stroke or exhaustion, such as rapid breathing, nausea, and headaches in yourself and others. You can hallucinate if you are dehydrated, so if you see something strange, ask a friend if they see it, too.

FOREST FIRES

A real threat on the mountains, forest fires are swift and deadly. You may not be able to safely outrun a fire, but climbing out of its reach is an option.

POISONING

Avoid buying any medicine, called "tonic" on the Trail, from people you don't trust or know. When you feel sick, always check with an adult for the right amount of medicine, so you do not poison yourself or fall ill from accidentally taking too much.

👉 FINDING YOUR WAY

Walking 2,000 miles (3,200 km) from Missouri to Oregon City in 1850 means there aren't roads or many signs. You have to navigate by landmarks along the way.

SOUTH PASS

This gently sloping pass marks the halfway point on the Oregon Trail and the location of the Continental Divide.

GREENWOOD CUTOFF

This shortcut saves a week of travel, but takes you through a scorching desert. The longer trip is advisable but the longer you are on the trail, the more risks you potentially face.

GREEN RIVER

This is one of the most dangerous river crossings on the Trail. Take the ferry instead of fording the river.

BIG HILL

Big Hill is one of the steepest hills on the Trail. A windlass, which allows you to mechanically crank up wagons without straining your animals, may be a good option. But a windlass has risks of its own.

SODA SPRINGS

A marvel of the Trail, Soda Springs is a fascinating place filled with naturally bubbling pools of carbonated water. Be careful though; some of the hot springs are extremely hot and can cause you serious burns!

SHOSHONE FALLS

You can hear these impressive and spectacular waterfalls from miles away.

THREE ISLAND CROSSING

This path across the Snake River involves strong currents and high waters. One option is to float your wagon across piece by piece, but that is a risky and often disastrous undertaking.

Look for these landmarks between Devil's Gate and Three Island Pass

DISTANCE FROM INDEPENDENCE, MISSOURI:

SOUTH PASS: 914 miles (1,471 km)

FORT BRIDGER: 1,026 miles (1,651 km)

SODA SPRINGS: 1,155 miles (1,859 km)

FORT HALL: 1,217 miles (1,959 km)

SHOSHONE FALLS: 1,337 miles (2,152 km)

The Oregon Trail™

THE ROAD TO OREGON CITY

The Oregon Trail™

GO WEST
Complete the Journey

You are a young settler headed out West by wagon train in the year 1850. You and your family are on the last leg of the dangerous frontier journey known as the Oregon Trail. You have crossed more than 1,300 miles of territory in what will later become the states of Kansas, Nebraska, Wyoming, and Idaho.

For fifteen miles a day for more than three months, you have walked beside your oxen and covered wagon with your family. You can't ride in the wagon because it holds everything you need for the journey and for your family's new lives as farmers in Oregon.

You've crossed mountains, deserts, and prairies, and you've passed through Devil's Gate and the perilous Snake River. You've also faced wild animals, dealt with raging forest fires, and learned how to survive in deadly desert conditions by traveling at night. You now know how to handle livestock and trade what you have. Best of all, there's still adventure ahead of you—*if* you can survive the steep and treacherous trek through areas like the hot, sandy Bruneau Dunes; the Cascade Rapids; the surging Columbia River; the bubbling Soda Springs; Fort Boise; Flagstaff Hill, which signals the start of the Blue Mountains; the Barlow Toll Road; and after that, the steep descent of Laurel Hill, near Mount Hood.

You've met indigenous people of various Nations like the Arapaho, Lakota, Shoshone, and Osage.

★ ★ ★

Only one path will lead you safely through this book to your destination, Oregon City, but there are twenty-three other possible endings, full of risks and surprises. Along the way, no matter what path you choose, you will experience natural disasters, sickness, and other hazards of the Trail.

You're trapped underneath the ice! How will you survive?

A deadly lynx is about to pounce!

Bandits are lurking nearby; what will you do?

Before you begin, make sure to read the Guide to the Trail at the back of the book, starting on page 326. It's filled with important information you'll need to make wise choices.

You're not alone, and you can make decisions with friends, people you meet along the way, or Ma and Pa—but also trust your good judgment. Use the resources you have, and you'll find your way to the end of the Trail at Oregon City, where you'll get your own plot of land to build a farmhouse and start a new life with your family!

Every second counts!
Think fast.
What will you do?

→ Ready? ←

BLAZE A TRAIL TO

OREGON CITY!

Three Island Crossing

AUGUST 31, 1850

You dip your hands into the warm water and splash it over your hot, sweaty face. It's so refreshing to wash the grime off your skin after being on the dusty trail that you can't help but smile.

The water is lapping at you like a soft, wet tongue . . . until suddenly you wake up, reach out, and feel something furry.

"Archie! Yuck!" you groan, pushing your dog away from where he's been licking your face.

Archie just looks at you with his big brown eyes and wags his tail.

"It's all right, boy." You laugh, scratching him around the ears as the five-a.m. bugle sounds. It's barely light outside your tent, but it's time to start the morning chores, eat breakfast, pack up your wagon, and get back on the Trail.

It's already been almost four months since you started your journey from Independence, Missouri, back in May. But every morning, it's a little harder to get up.

"Wake up, Samuel." You nudge your little brother, fast asleep beside you. "You need to milk Daisy."

"You do it," Samuel moans, rolling over on his feather mat.

Hannah, your little sister, marches into your tent. She's always been the earliest riser among you. Samuel used to be more energized in the morning, but as you've made your way through the difficult Rocky Mountains, he's needed more rest. Plus, instead of traveling fifteen miles a day, your wagon train has been covering only about ten to twelve miles because of the rugged and treacherous terrain.

"Ma says to hurry up," Hannah says, her bonnet sliding halfway over her eyes as usual.

"She needs you to get fuel for the fire, and Sam to milk—"

"Daisy," Samuel mutters, cutting her off. "I know, I know. I'm coming."

Hannah rolls her eyes at him and goes back to help Ma prepare breakfast. You don't blame Samuel for being grumpy as he packs up his bed and carries it out of the tent. Your body longs for more rest too. But you know you don't have that option. The wagon train will roll out in about an hour and a half, and you need to help Ma and Pa get everything ready.

Your stomach growls as you anticipate breakfast, which will probably be flapjacks and bacon . . . again. Since you've left Independence with a wagon led by a team of oxen piled high with everything you own, you've eaten more bacon than you ever dreamed was possible. Ma has been pretty creative with the few other foods you've carried with you for more than 1,400 miles so far: flour, cornmeal, sugar, coffee, salt, and beans. But it's still gotten boring. Luckily, you've also eaten whatever you have been able to catch along the Trail, including rabbits, squirrels, deer, and buffalo, along with fruits and berries.

"I can't wait to get to Oregon City and eat at a tavern again," Hannah says as if she is reading your mind.

"Me too, Hannah," you say. "If there even *are* any taverns."

Your family is traveling out West to claim the land available to anyone willing to make the trip. Other emigrants like you have already made it to Oregon City and started their lives. But you don't really know what to expect when you get there.

You've covered two-thirds of your trek, through prairie, desert, and now mountains. The sights along the way have been incredible, from steep cliffs to massive waterfalls to enormous rock formations, and more. And you've overcome a number of challenges, including dangerous river crossings, ferocious animals, and serious illnesses.

"Good morning," Caleb says as you walk past him with an armful of brush for the campfire. Caleb has proved to be an excellent wagon captain over the journey. His son and daughter, Joseph and Eliza, have become the best friends you've ever had.

"Good morning," you reply. "What's ahead on the Trail today?"

"We are going to have a meeting after we all fuel

up on breakfast," Caleb replies. "There's a big decision to make."

You feel a familiar tinge of excitement, wondering what the decision will be as you hurry back to your campsite and help Ma start a big fire. As the bacon starts sizzling in the iron skillet, you grind coffee beans and make a strong brew that everyone, even Hannah, drinks. You've all grown accustomed to drinking coffee on the Trail and are grateful it masks some of the bad-tasting water you are forced to use along the way.

Pa fixes you a plate of flapjacks, and you sink your teeth into a thick, buttery pancake. You wish there was some syrup but are grateful for your cow Daisy's steady supply of cream that Ma churns into butter by hanging a bucket on the side of the wagon as it bumps along the rocky terrain.

"Pa, do you know what big decision we have to make today?" you say.

"Yes. We need to choose whether or not to cross the Snake River two more times and head toward Fort Boise," Pa starts.

"That river again!" Hannah interrupts.

You shiver, remembering the ordeal you just went through at Three Island Crossing. You had never been more terrified than when Ma fell into the water, but luckily Pa was quick to save her.

"What's the other choice?" Samuel asks.

"We would take the South Alternate Route," Pa explains. "It goes south of the Snake River but runs along it, so you don't have to cross."

"Isn't that better, then?" Ma asks.

"I don't know," Pa answers. "It would take us through the Bruneau Sand Dunes. They are hot, dry, and dusty."

Your family sits quietly and ponders the options.

"I'm afraid to cross the river again," Ma says.

"Me too," adds Hannah.

"I'm worried about the dry conditions of the alternate route," Pa says. "It might be hard on the animals."

"And I hate being thirsty," Samuel adds, agreeing with Pa.

Everyone looks at you.

"It looks like you have to be the one to help us decide what we tell Caleb," Pa says. "What do you think we should do?"

You consider everything carefully. Even though the river crossings are dangerous, at least you know

what to expect. You're not sure what the dunes will be like. On the other hand, the idea of two more crossings is daunting.

What do you say?

If you pick the regular route, turn to page **294**

If you pick the alternate route, turn to page **264**

You sit in front of the fire and frantically rub your feet. Ma returns with the dishes.

"My goodness! How did this happen?" Ma says with a gasp when she spots your purple toes. You hold up a shoe and show her a worn sole. She takes it and walks over to Pa. You try wiggling your toes, but they are not moving as Pa rushes over to you.

"Does it hurt?" Pa asks.

"I can't really feel anything," you reply.

Pa nods at you and tries to smile, but he seems worried. He walks away to find the vet, the member of your wagon train with the most medical knowledge of the group. Ma sits with you and rubs your feet for a bit. After a few minutes, Pa returns with the vet, who presses firmly on your toes.

"Can you feel that?" the vet asks you.

"No," you respond, feeling scared.

The vet tells Pa to wrap your feet in a blanket and have you sit in front of the fire for the night. Ma bundles your feet tightly and you finally fall asleep, hoping that your feet will be back to normal by morning.

The bugle sounds, and you rush to unwrap your feet.

"Ma!" you shout, pointing to your feet, which are black all the way up to your ankles. Ma runs to get the vet, and soon a crowd is standing around you.

"This is terrible," the vet says. "But your feet can't be saved. If we don't remove them, you will lose your legs."

You start screaming before he finishes speaking.

Your family uses the rest of their money on supplies to help you heal after your surgery.

Oregon City is no longer in your future.

☞ **THE END**

You decide to give your parents time to recover
before making them continue on the journey. Even
if they were to rest in the wagon, there wouldn't be
room for both of them to lie down. Plus, you know
how bumpy and uncomfortable the ride would be.
And the truth is, the idea of leading your wagon
alone without Pa makes you nervous.

Hannah and Samuel help you do all the chores
that Ma and Pa usually do. You fix meals, but Pa is
still having trouble eating anything. It frightens you

to see his face so drawn and pale. Luckily, Ma seems to be improving slightly.

"I think your soup is making me stronger," she says with a weak smile.

Then, the next morning, Pa doesn't wake up. You hear Ma shouting and run over to where he is. You lean over to check whether he is breathing, but you can't hear anything.

"Pa!" you shout, shaking him. "Wake up, Pa!"

He remains motionless. You throw some water on his face to try to wake him up, but nothing happens.

"What do we do?" you finally cry, clinging to Ma.

Ma is barely strong enough to stand, but she tries everything to wake Pa. However, Pa doesn't open his eyes again. As night falls, you hear Ma sobbing in her tent and you realize that life as you know it has changed. Your body starts shaking as fear and grief fill your heart. How can you go on without Pa? Then it hits you. With Pa gone, you are in charge. Ma, Hannah, and Samuel are too beside themselves to make any decisions. You wish you could wake up and find that this is all a terrible nightmare. But it isn't. Your family is going to look to you now, so you try to think clearly and decide what to do. Do you head back to Fort Boise and try to find your way back to Kentucky, where you have family? Or do you push onward to Oregon and honor Pa's dream?

If you head back to Fort Boise, turn to page **301**

If you continue to Oregon, turn to page **209**

"I think we should camp," you say. "It'll be hard to keep walking and carry our things."

"And I'm too hungry," Hannah adds, while Samuel nods.

"Okay," Ma agrees, looking at all of you with concern. "I just hope we catch something soon."

Pa goes out to set the traps and try to hunt. But he comes back a few hours later with only one small bird.

"This is all I could catch, and I wasted a lot of bullets trying to catch things that weren't a good shot." He hangs his head.

Ma roasts the bird, and you each get a small piece. You savor every morsel and lick your fingers, still hungry. Poor Archie is left with the bones. His ribs are sticking out, and as you look at him, you wonder how skinny you must have gotten too.

The next morning, you hear hooves approaching. Pa draws his rifle, tensed. But it's fur trappers, who scour the area.

"It looks like you've fallen on hard times," one of the men says as he dismounts his horse.

"Yes, sir," Pa says. "I'm afraid we could use your help."

"I can help you hunt, and give you a bit of this dried buffalo jerky," the man offers.

Ma accepts the jerky gratefully and parcels it out to each of you. You try not to gobble it up and instead chew it slowly to make it last. Then Ma fixes coffee, and you each sip a nice hot cup. When you're done, your stomach doesn't feel as empty. But a few hours later, your stomach is rumbling again, and this time not because you're hungry. You end up getting severe cramps and diarrhea. Next comes vomiting and fever, and then the worst of all. You die of dysentery.

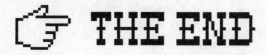 **THE END**

I think it might make the most sense to leave the wagon," you say, surprising yourself. The path has been so difficult and you're so close to Oregon City that you just want to get there as quickly as you can.

The rest of your family agrees and sorts through the things you will load onto the oxen. You take only your valuables, food, clothes, bedrolls, and essential cooking and camping supplies.

"I can't believe we're just leaving the wagon," Hannah says sadly.

"And all these things," Samuel adds, peering into it.

"Well, I have to say, I feel a bit lighter now," Pa says, trying to be cheerful. "And we should move much faster."

As Pa predicted, you are able to cover much more ground over the next few days. But soon you realize that your food supply is not going to get you to Oregon City.

"A few men are volunteering to scout for food while the rest remain camped," Caleb says to Pa. "What do you think?"

"Don't you think we should all stick together?" Ma asks, looking worried.

"I won't go if you don't want me to," Pa says, looking at all of you.

You exchange looks with Ma. Without saying a word, you know she feels the same as you. She doesn't want Pa to leave you behind, but at the same time she realizes the reasons he needs to go.

What do you say?

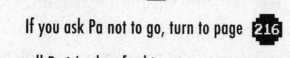

If you ask Pa not to go, turn to page 216

If you tell Pa it's okay for him to go, turn to page 230

Everyone wants to get out of the desert-like conditions as quickly as possible and votes for going through the dunes.

"Okay, so it looks like we have a hike ahead of us tomorrow," Caleb says. "Rest up, everybody."

"I'm too hot to rest," Samuel complains. "And I'm always thirsty."

You feel a rush of sympathy for your little brother, whose temperature is always running hotter than the rest of your family's. And you also have a small pang of guilt. He wasn't keen on coming this way all along and has been finding it difficult.

"I have a piece of honey candy," Joseph offers Samuel. "Will that help?"

Samuel takes the candy gratefully and sucks on it in silence as you help to prepare camp.

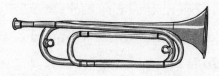

The next morning when the early bugle sounds, everyone gets ready for the day's hike through the dunes. If all goes well, you should be well across them by your midday break.

Everything goes smoothly for a while. The animals pull the wagons without a hitch, and Pa smiles, pleased with the progress. But when you reach halfway up the dunes, your wagon is stuck! The oxen keep pulling the wagon and straining, but it won't budge. And when Pa tries to help push it out, it just sinks deeper into the sand.

Finally, with a tremendous amount of effort,

the wagon is freed. But in the process, your animals are overworked, and they don't recover. Soon, their carcasses line the Trail, and you are left stranded. It's too hard to go on without them, and you can't carry everything you need for the journey on your backs. Pa decides to stop at the next trading post and try to get some more oxen. If you're lucky, you might find some go-backers willing to sell you theirs. But until then, your trip is on hold.

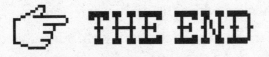

☞ THE END

I agree," Pa says. "Let's use the rope to set traps."

You spend the rest of the afternoon making traps with Pa and are proud when you put together four strong ones. Pa asks you to come with him to set them, and you bait each with a small piece of bacon.

As night falls, Pa says it's time to check on the traps. You turn over the first three traps and find nothing. As you approach the fourth trap, you hear something struggling inside and smile at Pa.

"Sounds like a good dinner," he says. You hear a rustling and wonder if there's another small animal nearby. But it's a mountain lion! You scream and try to run, but you don't get very far.

 **THE END**

Everyone agrees to push through the snowstorm, since the idea of sitting around in the freezing cold and wind and waiting for it to pass seems more dangerous. Instead, you all bundle up in extra layers of clothes to keep warm, and drape all the extra blankets over the oxen. Pa feeds the animals handfuls of grain to help calm them down and give them energy to keep moving.

You trudge through the snow, amazed by how quickly everything around you is covered in a sheet of white. The cold wind is chapping any part of your skin that is exposed. Even though your scarf is wrapped around your head and much of your face, the part of your nose peeking through is freezing.

"This must be what it feels like to be a snowman," Hannah says, hugging herself for warmth as she struggles to keep up with you.

"I know," you say, imagining that your nose is as bright as a carrot.

"I wish we could play in the snow instead of having to walk all day," she says, looking wistful.

"Yeah, it's no fun to have snow if we can't even play in it," Samuel adds.

"Maybe we can play for a little while when we make camp," you say.

"If I'm not completely frozen by then," Hannah complains.

"It'll be even better if you are," you say, picking up a handful of snow and tossing it at her gently. "Snowmen are supposed to be cold, right?"

Hannah sticks out her tongue playfully and runs back to the wagon for a rest, huddling inside it with Archie for warmth.

As you hike for the next couple of hours, the wind and snow ease up and then taper off completely. By the time you stop to make camp, the sun is shining again. You help Pa set up the tents, and Ma builds a roaring fire. The animals are fed and left to recover, and then you finally have time to play until supper.

"Let's have a snowball fight," Joseph says. "We'll pick teams."

"Yeah!" Samuel says. "I want to play."

Joseph and you are the team leaders. You form your teams and then split up to plan. You pick Samuel and Eliza.

"Let's make a hundred snowballs and have them ready to use," Samuel says.

"And then let's go around that way, and plan a sneak attack on the other team," you say, pointing in the direction away from camp.

You see Joseph hiding behind a tree and decide to get him first. Samuel gives you the signal that the coast is clear. Crouching down so you can't be seen, you run around in a wide circle so he won't see you coming. You're holding two of the biggest snowballs you've ever made. As you're running, your footsteps sink into the freshly fallen snow, leaving big footprints. But then you suddenly step into a frozen pond without realizing it. With a crunch, the thin layer of ice gives way and . . .

SPLASH!

You plunge into the icy water!

Instinctively, you gasp as you fall and take in a huge breath of air before your head goes underwater.

But now you are trapped underneath the ice and have only a few minutes to act before you will run out of air.

Don't panic, you tell yourself. You look up and attempt to find the hole in the ice where you fell in. That way, you can try to climb out of it again. Underwater, the ice all looks the same to you, until you notice a darker spot to your left and a lighter spot to your right.

Which one do you slowly move toward so you can try to pull yourself out of the water?

If you move toward the darker spot, turn to page **292**

If you move toward the lighter spot, turn to page **309**

Seeing Samuel looking so cozy curled up with Archie only reminds you of how freezing you are. With that one small ember still glowing in the campfire, you grab a couple of nearby twigs and gently place them into the pit. You can put out the fire after you've warmed yourself up just a bit. You know that starting a fire when everyone else is asleep could be incredibly dangerous, but right now, you're too cold to think of anything but warming up. You blow on the embers softly to ignite the flames, but nothing happens for several minutes.

Finally, your work pays off when you see the embers glowing a warm yellow-white. Soon enough, small flames tickle the branches. You hurry to grab more kindling before the twigs die out completely, because you haven't even had a chance to really warm yourself up.

After you pile on branch after branch, watching the flames lick around the burning wood, you finally have a roaring fire that crackles and glows in the dark. You hold your trembling hands near the edge of the campfire, enjoying the way the heat travels through your fingertips to the rest of your chilled body.

But you're so exhausted, and you desperately want to lie down. Sitting on the cold, hard ground isn't entirely pleasant, even with the fire. You grab your mat and drag it over to the campfire, placing it alongside the pit to receive the greatest amount of warmth. Once you lie down, you enjoy the  heat radiating off the flames. Before you know it, you burrow down into your mat and drift off to sleep.

You're jolted awake by the smell of smoke and the stench of something burning. You have fallen asleep too close to the fire, and no one is awake to help you.

☞ THE END

We'll make camp and wait out the storm," Pa says, glancing at the clouds with a worried expression. "I just hope it passes quickly."

You help him set up the tents, struggling to get them to stand up. It's too windy to start a fire, so you eat a cold supper of prairie biscuits and jerky. And then you ask Ma if you can play in the snow.

"Okay," she says. "But not for too long. It'll be dark soon."

You, Hannah, and Samuel build a giant snow fort and hide behind it, piling up an arsenal of snowballs. Joseph and Eliza do the same on the other side of camp.

"Charge!" Joseph shouts, and the battle begins. Snowballs fill the air as you pelt one another. The cold snow stings your skin, and you finally call a truce when both sides are out of snowballs. You run in the snow and fall over, laughing.

"Let's make snow angels!" Hannah says, lying down next to you and waving her arms and legs in the snow.

"Come on back now," Ma calls.

You go back to the tents and only realize how cold it is once you've stopped running around. Even though you try to warm up under the blankets, as it gets darker, the temperature drops and you are really cold.

"I'm freezing," Samuel whines. "I can't sleep."

"Me either," Hannah adds.

Ma looks concerned.

"I was going to put these blankets on the oxen, but you better use them," she says.

Finally, huddled together, you are able to get to sleep.

By morning, the snow has stopped falling. You step out of the tent, and the thick blanket of snow reaches above your knees as you walk. After only a few moments, you hear shouting.

"The oxen!"

It's Pa! You rush over to where he is and find him looking distraught.

"Half of them have perished," he says, sounding devastated. "What will we do?"

The remaining oxen won't be able to pull the weight of the wagon on their own. Other wagons have lost animals too.

"We should have kept moving through the storm," Caleb says, sounding regretful. "We'll just have to take what we can carry on the animals. There's no other choice."

Even though you are filled with sadness over the lost animals, there's no time to waste. You spend the next few hours helping your parents sort through your things, choosing only the most important items to take with you.

While Ma and Pa are trying to attach bags to the remaining oxen and onto Daisy, Samuel runs over to you.

"Hannah and I found some wild berries," he says. "Come see!"

You follow Samuel and run over to some bushes in the distance. As you approach, you see Hannah pulling berries off the bush and filling up her apron. She looks up at you and smiles.

"Look how many I have," she says. "I hope they are good to eat."

Just then you spot something moving behind the bush. It's a bear!

You freeze, terrified. It feels like everything is happening more slowly than it really is  as the bear comes toward Hannah. You're afraid that it wants the berries and will attack her, and you have only a moment to react. Do you pick up Hannah's doll from where it is lying on the ground near you and throw it at the bear to distract it? Or do you yell for Hannah to run?

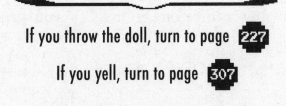

If you throw the doll, turn to page **227**

If you yell, turn to page **307**

The taste of fresh honey is too mouthwatering to resist. You relent and agree to let Joseph smoke out the bees. Joseph finds a large, heavy stick and sets it on fire, then douses the flames with his foot, creating a smoking log. He holds it up to you.

"Here, take this while I climb," he orders.

You hesitate. The bees are already swarming around you. Still, you take the smoking stick. Joseph jumps to clamber up the tree, his movements shaking the nest even more than yours first did. A bee whizzes by your ear.

"Joseph, I don't think this is a good idea," you say nervously.

"I'm almost there," he grunts. "Do you want honey or not?"

"Joseph," says Eliza, "I think we should just get down."

But Joseph ignores her and grabs the smoking branch. He holds it up to the nest. The smoke clouds the nest, and the humming increases to a dull roar.

"Joseph!" Eliza shouts. "Stop it!"

"Just calm down!" Joseph says, but he also sounds scared.

You scramble to climb down, too frightened of the bees buzzing around your head. But as you reach for a branch, something stings the back of your neck.

"They're stinging me!" you shout.

"Me too!" Eliza and Joseph cry out.

As the three of you tumble to the ground, your eyes feel puffy, and you can't catch your breath. You look down at your fingers and see that they're swelling up.

You have an allergic reaction to the bee stings. Your journey ends here.

☞ **THE END**

The idea of floating down the rapids on a raft sounds too dangerous to everyone in your family. You decide the Barlow Toll Road sounds safer, even if that means spending the extra money and facing the steep hill. It's worth it to avoid the risk of capsizing into the icy cold waters of the Columbia River. You shiver, remembering how cold you were in the pond you fell into. The last thing you want is anything even remotely close to that dreadful experience.

Most of the families agree and plan to follow the Barlow route and pay the toll at the end. A couple of others decide to risk the rapids. You wish them luck and leave them as they start building rafts. You hope to see them again in Oregon City before too long.

If all goes well on the toll road, you should be in Oregon City in about two weeks. As your family makes its way down the path Barlow carved, the first stop is the Tygh Valley, where you make camp. You have entered the famous Cascade Mountain range now, and the path is steep and treacherous at times.

"The tollgate is coming up," Pa says as you make camp. "We should reach it tomorrow."

As promised, you arrive at Barlow's Gate the next day after a long trek through the mountains. The station there is a welcome change, and Ma is pleased to find fruit available for sale. Your food supplies have slowly been dwindling, and you are down to the basics now. Ma has been careful to make sure everyone gets enough to eat to replenish their energy but nothing extra. She's afraid that you will run out before the journey ends if you have any delays.

"This almost makes paying the toll worth it,"

Ma says with a smile as she shows you the apples she selected. "I'm going to make a pie with these tonight."

The pie is delicious, but it doesn't make up for the grueling travel through the mountains. After hours of climbing, you are hungrier than ever. You pass the time dreaming of the big meals you will enjoy in Oregon City. You know you will sit down to a table loaded with all your favorite foods. It's been nothing but beans, bacon, and pan bread for weeks now.

"We are approaching Laurel Hill," Caleb declares after two more days of exhausting climbs. This is the steep hill you were warned about.

"How in the world will we get down there?" Ma asks, looking at the tremendously sharp descent.

You think back to Alcove Spring, at the beginning of the Trail, where the men of the train used their collective strength to lower the wagons down the challenging incline. That seems like much longer than five months ago. And with everyone as worn out and exhausted as they are, it's probably not a good idea.

"We could lower the wagons with ropes," a woman suggests. "Tie them securely to trees first."

She explains that you would lead the animals down separately, after loading as much as you could onto them.

"Or we could cut some of the biggest trees down and tie them to the backs of the wagons," a man says.

You wonder what that would do.

"The weight of the trees would create enough drag on the wagons to stop them from rolling too quickly and bumping into the animals," he explains.

Both options sound risky. As expected, there are lots of opinions about which to choose, and the debate grows intense. Finally, Caleb makes everyone quiet down.

"We'll vote," he says, "and settle it that way."

There are seven wagons left in your group. Three choose the ropes, and three others choose to cut down the trees.

"Your family is the tiebreaker," Caleb says, turning to Ma and Pa. "What do you want to do?"

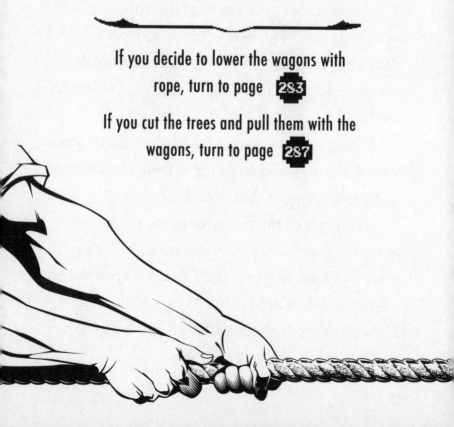

If you decide to lower the wagons with rope, turn to page **283**

If you cut the trees and pull them with the wagons, turn to page **287**

You can't imagine turning back at this point.
Pa brought you so far, and to return to Kentucky
without him would be even more heartbreaking than
continuing. You're more determined than ever to
make it to Oregon City.

You tell Ma your decision, and she nods. She
looks so frail, it frightens you. As it grows later in
the day, you hear horses approaching and freeze. You
aren't sure whether to run and get Pa's rifle or sit still
and wait to see who it is. While you are hesitating,
two men become visible.

"You all need some help?" one of them asks. From
the looks of them, you guess they are fur traders.

"Yes, please," Ma speaks up before you have a
chance. "My husband passed away, and we need help
getting to Oregon City. I can pay you."

The men look at each other and then back at Ma.

"Sure, ma'am," the same man says, and then they
help you bury Pa, which is the hardest thing you've
ever had to do in your life.

Later, you hear the men talking to each other, after they check out your wagon and your animal team. Then they return to you and Ma.

"We'll need a fee of two hundred dollars to get you to Oregon City from here," the man who seems to be in charge says.

Two hundred dollars! You feel yourself get hot with anger. Who has that kind of money to spare? You take Ma aside.

"That is robbery," you whisper. "I think they are taking advantage of us."

"What choice do we have?" Ma says. "I'll give them my jewelry to get us to Oregon City safely."

Pa gave Ma those jewels, and he would want her to have them. But he would also feel more comfortable if you weren't alone on the Trail.

What do you tell the men?

If you say it's a deal, turn to page **274**

If you say you will go on your own, turn to page 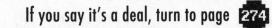 **276**

Pa looks at you all.

"Are you sure?" he asks.

"Yes," Ma says, speaking for all of you. "We will go down the Columbia River."

You know it isn't an easy thing for Ma to agree to, especially since even simple river crossings have always made her nervous. This is a bit more complicated and potentially more dangerous. But at least this time you will be traveling on a raft. And by taking this route, you can avoid the toll road and the dangers of the Barlow route.

While Pa goes to tell Caleb and the rest of the wagon train about your decision, you check out your surroundings with Joseph and Eliza.

"I wonder why this area is called The Dalles," you say, expecting Joseph to give one of his usual detailed answers. But he just shrugs, and Eliza pipes up instead.

"Pa told me the French named it because of the way the land is shaped like a big trough," she says. "*Dalles* is the word for 'trough' in French."

You imagine explorers coming from as far as France to see what you're looking at now. And here you are, finally on the last part of your journey to Oregon City. Amazing!

When Pa returns, he tells you the plan.

"Only a few of the families are going with us," he explains. "The rest are taking the Barlow Toll Road."

You feel a pang of concern. What if you made the wrong decision?

"But don't worry," Pa continues, as if he is reading your mind. "I'm going to build us a nice strong raft, and we will be fine."

Pa's carpentry skills have been a huge asset on this trip, and once again they will be put to use.

"I'll have to cut down several of those tall trees to start," he tells you. "And then I'll shape them into planks and lash them together to make the raft."

The raft will have to be strong enough to carry your wagon, the animals, and your family down the river. It's a big job, but you're confident Pa can do it. But first, you will all make camp and get a good night's rest.

The next morning, Caleb approaches your family's campfire at breakfast with some news.

"Several men from the nearby Wasco Nation have offered to help us across the river," he says.

"Do they have a ferry?" Pa asks. "I haven't heard of it."

"Not exactly a ferry," Caleb continues. "But they take people across in large canoes."

"Why would we want to do that?" Pa asks. "I'm going to build the raft, which will be big enough for all of us."

"They have a lot of experience with the river, so it might be safer," Caleb says. "But they won't be able to take your whole family at once. You'd have to break up."

Ma and Pa exchange looks. You know they don't like the idea of splitting you up. But traveling on the canoes would mean less weight for the raft to carry. The Wasco people are friendly, Caleb says, but they would need some goods in exchange for their help.

What do you decide?

If you ask the Wasco Nation for help, turn to page 284

If you decide to stick to your own raft, turn to page 261

I don't want you to go," you tell Pa, knowing Ma feels the same.

Pa nods, almost relieved. "I think that's the right choice." He smiles, looking proud. "If we separate, it could be much worse and—"

A cold gust of wind interrupts Pa and pushes a flurry of snow into the wagon train. The temperature dramatically drops, and snow fills the air.

"It's snowing!" yells Hannah, bouncing up and down.

"Bizarre to see snow this time of year," says Caleb, turning to Pa. "I agree that if we get lost, it'll be hard to find our way back to the camp. All this snow doesn't help matters much either."

"Then let's continue on," says Pa. "We'll stay near the camp and hunt."

"Maybe Joseph and I can trap some rabbits," you suggest.

"Good thinking," Pa says.

You shoulder your heavy pack and continue on through the fresh snow, the weight somehow feeling a little lighter knowing that Pa won't be out there on his own, leaving you behind.

Your group has wandered higher into the Blue Mountains, where the trees are sparser and it's easier to navigate. The snow is loose and powdery beneath your feet. Suddenly, you hear something that sounds like thunder overhead. Thunderstorms aren't unheard of in the middle of winter, but this sounds different, closer somehow. It's as if the whole earth is shaking beneath your feet.

"Avalanche!" shouts Caleb. "Try to find cover in the trees!"

But the snow is barreling down too quickly on you and the other families, and the thick trees are too far down the mountain. Chaos overtakes everyone, and all you can see is that white powder crashing down toward you.

☞ **THE END**

You all agree that the best choice is to go around the dunes, rather than try to pass through them. The wagon train slowly makes its way around the massive mounds of sand. You look up at them, impressed by how winds piled up these huge hills over time, to the point where they stand hundreds of feet high. And even more impressive is how they don't just blow away.

As you hike, Caleb tells everyone that there are

hot springs coming up after a few days' hike, and that perks up the mood a bit. You remember the fun everyone had back at the Soda Springs, where there were geysers and a spring that fizzed and bubbled like soda. That would be refreshing right now!

As you leave the dunes, your wagon train passes several beautiful areas, including a lake and canyons. There's good hunting, too, with plenty of antelope and birds. Caleb halts the wagons every now and then when someone spots a good hunting opportunity.

You're near a canyon, and during the next break, Ma says it's okay to go exploring for a little while. Eliza has always loved to climb, and you scramble up the side of a big cliff with her, ready to see what's at the top.

"Hurry up!" Eliza says, ahead of you. You race after her, happy to feel the breeze on your face. It's a clear, sunny day and one of the nicest you've had in a long time.

When you get to the top of the cliff, the view of the canyon is spectacular.

"Oh, look!" Eliza says, and you turn, expecting her to point out something in the scenery. But instead it's a little kitten, peeking its head out from behind a rock.

"It's so cute," you say with a smile for the orange cat with huge green eyes.

"Here, kitty," Eliza beckons, holding her hand out to the tiny cat. But it just stays where it is, motionless.

"Don't be scared," Eliza continues, taking a few steps closer. "I won't hurt you." She bends, making herself smaller and less threatening.

But when she reaches the kitten and tries to pet it, the frightened cat swats her paw and scratches Eliza on the face. Eliza recoils, covering her cheek, and doesn't watch where she is stepping. She slips and stumbles off the edge of the cliff!

"Eliza!" you shout, imagining your friend

plummeting to the ground, hundreds of feet below. You rush to the edge, terrified, and find Eliza clinging to a rock an arm's length below you.

"Hold on!" you say, your heart racing as you wonder what to do. Do you lean forward and reach out your hand for her to hold on to? Then you can use all your strength to pull her up. Or do you try to find a sturdy branch for her to grab? That might be easier, but it means she will have to wait, and you don't know how long she will be able to hold on. What do you do?

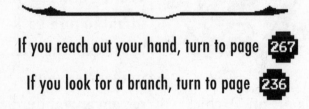

If you reach out your hand, turn to page **267**

If you look for a branch, turn to page **236**

You slowly turn your body away from the lynx, pivoting on your toes so you don't make any sudden moves. Archie is still facing the wildcat, staring at it.

"Okay, Archie, on the count of three, we are going to make a break for it," you say in a whisper.

"One. Two. Three. Let's go, boy!" you shout as you start in a dead sprint toward camp. Archie follows right behind you. Your heart is beating fast, and you're afraid to turn back to check if the lynx is coming after you.

"Come on, Archie!" you scream as you hurdle over small branches that have fallen to the ground. You're churning your legs faster than you ever have before. Suddenly you see Archie stumble in a small ditch.

"Get up!" you shout as Archie twists his body to get back up. But the lynx is on top of him! You watch in horror as the wildcat bites into the side of Archie's neck. His paws swat the lynx in the face, and Archie barks so loudly that it seems to startle the cat. After several more growls, the lynx spots a deer in the distance and takes off after it. You rush toward Archie to help him, and he is whimpering. You lift him into your arms and carry him back to camp. There, the vet bandages up Archie to prevent him from losing more blood.

A few weeks pass, and Archie's wounds have healed, though he doesn't seem quite like himself. You decide to play fetch—maybe that will cheer him up. As you are about to throw the stick, Archie bites down on your arm.

You yell in agony. The vet from camp runs to your side.

"Were you bit?" the vet asks.

"It was just Archie," you explain.

The next day is one of the saddest of your life as you help Pa bury Archie, who, despite all your hopes, died suddenly in the night. You make a marker out of a big stone, and Hannah sprinkles wildflowers on top. You don't want to leave without Archie, but you have to continue, and you leave his grave with a heavy heart and tears in your eyes.

Over the next few days, you have nausea and don't feel like eating anything. Everyone thinks you are just reacting to the death of Archie.

Ma tries to give you some special foods, but you have trouble swallowing, and you start to feel confused. A few days later, you are foaming at the mouth. You die of rabies.

☞ **THE END**

You pick up the doll and fling it in the direction of the bear. The bear pounces and starts to chew on it while you, Hannah, and Samuel run back to camp. You think you've escaped but then realize that the bear has followed you!

"Run!" you yell to everyone in the camp. "Bear!"

Everyone runs and hides behind a tree. But you watch in horror as the bear ravages your food supply. Ma and Pa had just packed up your food for the remaining oxen to carry. Now the bear feasts on the bacon and sugar and tears through the bags of flour. By the time he finally lumbers away, satisfied, everything is destroyed.

"We're ruined," Ma cries, clutching you as if she doesn't have the strength to stand on her own. "What will we do now?"

You just gulp, speechless. Now you have no wagon

and hardly any food. The rest of the wagon train offers to share what they have, but no one has much extra to spare. They all have to think of their own survival.

Over the next couple of days, your family is forced to kill another one of your oxen for food. When you think about it, you feel sad, but there's no other choice. Even though you were tired of flapjacks, corn cakes, and bacon before, you desperately wish for them now.

As the ox meat runs out, Ma rations meals even more strictly. When you camp, Pa lays traps for small animals, but it's hard to catch anything. You continue to look for berries and fruits with the rest of the kids. But soon the gnawing feeling of hunger starts to become familiar and it's harder to keep walking each day, especially climbing through the mountains.

"I think we should camp for a while so I can try to hunt," Pa says.

"But if we keep going, we might find some food or a trading post up ahead," Ma argues.

"Maybe another train will come by with more food to share," Pa says.

"We can't ask anyone for their food." Ma shakes her head.

"But they might have extra that they are willing to trade with us," Pa replies, trying to sound hopeful.

You listen to your parents debate what to do and try not to feel afraid. Finally, they turn to you.

"What do you think we should do?" they ask.

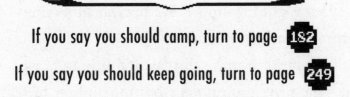

If you say you should camp, turn to page **182**

If you say you should keep going, turn to page **249**

I'll take care of everything while you're gone if you want to go, Pa," you say, trying to sound brave.

"Thank you," Caleb says to you, with an approving nod. "I think this will be the best bet for everyone."

Caleb, Pa, and a couple of other men from the wagon train take off. As you watch them leave, you feel a little anxious but hopeful that everything will be okay.

That night for supper, Ma fixes small servings of cornmeal hash and beans.

"We need to make this last for as long as we can," she says. You eat your portion and try to tell yourself that you are satisfied as you help do all of Pa's chores.

At night, you wake up to a terrible sound. The oxen are moaning and grunting in a desperate way. You remain in your tent, frozen with fear. Something is attacking them, and it could attack you and your family, too! You have to stay quiet and inside. There's nothing you can do about it.

In the morning, you see that the oxen have been badly injured by some kind of wild animal. They are not going to make it.

Pa returns a few hours later and surveys the dying animals sadly.

"There was no trading post for miles around here," he says. "Maybe if I had been here, I could have saved the oxen."

Your family will continue to push on with what little you can carry on your backs. You take all the food you have, but soon you will run out of food completely.

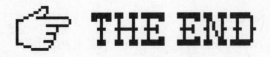 **THE END**

You drop the dirt onto the glowing orange ember and watch it as it turns to black. Then you stomp on the ashes just to make sure the fire is completely out. You've heard of enough fires accidentally burning down camps that you don't want to take any chances. Instead, you go to the wagon and grab one of the quilts that Ma has sewn on the journey. She's made several and has used them to barter for goods along the way. Back in your tent, wrapped snugly in the thick quilt, you're finally able to fall into a deep sleep.

Before you know it, the morning bugle sounds.

"It's already morning?" you mumble as you crawl out of bed, feeling envious that Samuel seems far more rested than you.

You feel like you are dragging as everyone sets out to do the morning chores. Samuel milks Daisy as usual, while Hannah pulls out the dishes for breakfast and grinds coffee. You walk over to the woods to collect firewood, glad that it's so easy to find fuel in this heavily forested area.

Archie follows you, wagging his tail happily.

"*Now* you're with me, instead of last night, when I could have used your help," you say, throwing a small twig, which Archie eagerly runs to fetch and bring back to you.

Playing with Archie wakes you up, and you end up moving a bit farther from camp than you expected. But it feels good to race with Archie in the crisp early-morning air, and you're starting to feel a bit more energized.

"I guess I should start gathering some branches," you finally say aloud. "I don't want to keep breakfast waiting."

Just then, your dog freezes, and you hear a low growl emerge from him.

"What is it, boy?" you ask as you glance around with concern. But you don't see anything alarming nearby.

Archie continues to stare at something and growl. You try to see what is bothering him and squint toward the trees. *Yikes!* Blending in with the branches of a tree is something that makes your heart skip a beat.

It's a lynx! A giant gray lion-like cat is staring straight at you, watching your every move. Its gray eyes are piercing, and its long hair almost forms a beard. Frozen, you stare back at the big cat. You've heard about these beautiful but dangerous creatures, but you have never seen one before in real life.

"Hush, Archie," you whisper softly as your heart races. The cat's ears are twitching, and you wonder if it is feeling threatened by Archie. All its muscles seem tensed, like it might be ready to leap at any second. Is it going to attack you? You know that lynxes move very quickly and are powerful, and you don't want to get in the way of this one's sharp claws.

You try to stay calm and think about what you should do, even as you feel your heartbeat pounding in your throat. Your gut reaction is to run back to camp as quickly as you can, but you don't know if it will chase you. Another option is to try to scare the lynx away by yelling, throwing rocks at it, and waving your arms around. But what if that just makes it angry and encourages it to attack?

What do you do?

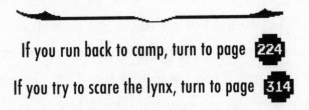

If you run back to camp, turn to page **224**

If you try to scare the lynx, turn to page **314**

Your eyes scan the ground for a branch that is long
and strong enough to support Eliza's weight.

"Hold on, Eliza!" you say in a panicked voice,
while rifling through several branches. Finally, you
find one that should work and run back to where
she is still clinging to the rock. The branch extends
just far enough for her to grab on to it. With all your
might, you are able to pull your friend back up safely.

"Thanks. I thought I was a goner." Eliza gasps,
trying to catch her breath. You sit for a few moments,
thinking about what could have happened. Then you
change the subject, talking about the cat, which has
already run away.

"We should get going," you finally say, pulling
Eliza to her feet. "Everyone must be waiting for us."

Over the next few days, your wagon train makes
its way over to the hot springs. Even though everyone
is excited about the change, they are also worried
about how much food you have left. Late in your
journey, supplies are running low. When you set out
from Independence, Missouri, you never thought it

would be possible to run out of bacon, but there isn't even much of that left now.

When you finally arrive at the hot springs, Caleb says you will make camp for a couple of days and rest. Ma is ready to wash your filthy clothes, and all the kids are tasked with helping. As you help Ma scrub while Hannah and Samuel fetch more water, Pa sits down next to both of you and discusses your food situation.

"I'm afraid we're not just running out of food, but we're getting short on supplies, also," Pa says.

"What do you mean?" you ask.

Pa pulls some rope out from his back pocket.

"This is all the rope we have left, and I am not

sure when we are going to get to another trading post for me to get more supplies before Oregon City."

You think about all the ways you use rope on this trip and how important it is.

"I was just asking Ma if I should use what rope we have left to make traps to try to catch some small animals tonight," Pa continues. "Or she could weave it into a fishing net."

The idea of some fresh game or fish makes your stomach grumble. You've gotten good at setting traps with Joseph since the very first time you caught jackrabbits at the beginning of the Trail. But sometimes fish are easier to catch, if it's a good spot on the river. What do you recommend?

If you suggest making traps, turn to page **189**

If you suggest making a net, turn to page **251**

Joseph, we need to get back," you say. "It's probably time to get rolling again, and we haven't eaten yet."

Joseph looks a little bit annoyed.

"Come on, Joseph," Eliza adds. "The last thing we need is to get stung by bees. You know Pa would be upset if we got hurt."

"I guess you're right," Joseph agrees reluctantly. "I've never actually smoked bees out of a hive before, anyway."

That makes you laugh. Joseph is always filled with facts about everything and knows a lot about all sorts of things. And he also has a lot of good ideas. But sometimes he is a little overconfident, too. You're fine with giving up the honey and heading back to the wagons. Besides, you know that you have Fort Boise to look forward to in the next week. Ma usually lets you get some kind of small treat at the trading posts.

Over the next few days, everyone's patience is tested as the anticipation of getting to Fort Boise grows. You haven't passed a trading post for three weeks!

"I can't wait to get to the fort," Hannah says, walking with you as she swings her worn rag doll by the arm. "I'm going to get a new dress for my doll."

You look at Hannah's own dress and dirty apron and think about the last time you were able to wash your clothes and have a proper bath. You know how raggedy you must look too, just like everyone else in the wagon train.

As you walk, you kick a pebble and notice your dilapidated shoes, which have been repaired several

times already since Ma bought them for you back in
Independence. From walking so many miles a day,
they are growing paper-thin again and need new
soles.

When you finally arrive at Fort Boise, everyone
perks up at the welcoming scene. Several other wagon
trains are parked in corrals—circles to protect their
animals and keep out thieves and predators. There's
the bustle of people trading and making repairs to
their wagons. People from the Paiute, Nimi'ipuu, and
Shoshone Nations offer goods for sale, while kids run
around and play.

After you make camp and have supper, Ma gives
you permission to explore a little on your own.

"You know this is the last trading post before we
get to Oregon City," she says. "This is our last chance
to buy anything we need for the rest of the journey.
Go look carefully."

You take Samuel and Hannah by the hands and
walk around. A group of Nimi'ipuu people have
spread out their wares, which include woven blankets,
beads, and skins. But as Hannah stops to admire a

carved wooden horse, you notice some tall moccasin boots lined with fur.

"These are good for snow," a Nimi'ipuu man says to you.

You politely admire how neatly the leather is stitched and move on.

Another merchant has some rock candy on sticks. The colorful crystals of sugar in jagged shapes form long lollipops. He also has honey candy and molasses for sale that make your mouth water.

When you get back, Ma is discussing what items to get with Pa. She explains that you have enough of the essential foods you need to get to Oregon City. Pa tells her he has completed all the wagon repairs for the rough, rocky, and snowy mountains ahead. And he's purchased any available spare parts.

"We have a little extra money to let the kids get something," she says.

"Can I get the wooden horse toy?" Hannah asks with a pleading look, forgetting about her rag doll's new dress.

"Let's see how much it costs," Pa says with

a smile. Each of you left behind all your toys in Kentucky, and you rarely ask for anything.

"Is there anything you need?" Ma asks you. "If not, I might get us a jar of molasses and extra sugar."

Your mouth starts to water as you think of the molasses. It's been so long since you've had Ma's famous delicious molasses pudding. But you can feel the pebbles underfoot and wonder if you should mention how worn out your shoes are, especially with the hardest part of the mountains ahead of you.

What do you say?

If you say she should get the molasses and sugar, turn to page **304**

If you say your shoes need repair, turn to page **268**

You can go, but be safe, and we will see you on the other side," Ma says while giving you a hug. Pa places his hand on your shoulder.

"Listen to everything Caleb tells you," he says. You wave goodbye to Samuel, Hannah, and Archie and run back to Caleb with Joseph and Eliza.

"Okay, team, this will be challenging. But if we work together, we should have no problems," Caleb says with a smile. You smile back, then line up next to the animals and help guide them as you start walking.

Your trip around the mountain is difficult. The animals keep trying to veer off the path, and you constantly have to stop and wait for them to line up again. After several hours, you are able to cover some ground.

"I wonder if they are already across and waiting for us," you say to Caleb.

"They should be by now, but they will definitely be there by the time we reach the other side," he replies.

Finally, you are around the mountain and on the

other side of the rapids. You're so excited to tell Pa that you helped save one of the oxen from falling off the side of a cliff. But when you walk around to the mouth of the rapids, no one is there.

"Where are they?" you ask with a sinking feeling.

Caleb looks just as worried as you.

"Let's give them some more time. I'm sure they will be here soon," he replies in a hopeful voice.

You sit staring at the rapids for hours, but there is no sign of your family or anyone else. In the distance, Caleb sees pieces of the raft floating and banging up against the rocks. As night falls, you know that your family is not coming and you are now on your own. Caleb, Joseph, and Eliza try comforting you, but you just want to be alone. You are numb and can't speak. A couple of days later, you have no choice but to continue on with Caleb and his family.

☞ **THE END**

You grab the kettle of warm water and pour it into a bucket. Then you stick your feet inside.

"What are you doing?" Ma asks as she returns with the dishes.

"Look at my feet," you say.

Ma looks at your feet and runs to get the vet, who is the closest thing to a doctor you have in your wagon train.

"It looks like you have a bit of frostbite on your feet," the vet says after taking a look.

"What is going to happen to me?" you ask, feeling scared.

"We'll see," he says. "But you did the right thing to soak your feet in warm water. Do that for a while longer and then wrap them up warmly."

You follow his instructions and in the morning unwrap the blanket covering your feet. Your toes have mostly returned to their normal color, except for the big and pinky toes on both feet. They are an unslightly shade of black.

When the vet sees them, he shakes his head.

"I'm afraid these toes have gangrene. We'll have to remove them so it doesn't spread to the rest of your feet."

You're devastated, but you try to be brave about losing your toes. Ma can't stop crying and seems even more upset than you. Over the next week, she and Pa decide to head south to California. They think it might be an easier trail for you to travel than Oregon. All because of your shoddy shoes, your family's dreams of Oregon are given the boot.

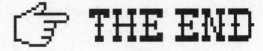 THE END

I think we should keep going," you say, and Ma nods in agreement. "We can still hunt for food, but maybe we will find a trading post."

"I guess you're right," Pa agrees. "But it isn't going to be easy." He gives everyone in the family a load to carry. It's mostly your bedrolls, waterskins, and a few other essential items, but it's still heavy. Pa takes the biggest load for himself, carrying his rifle, ammunition, and camping supplies.

It's hard to keep moving with the bag strapped to your back. You don't want to complain, but your shoulders hurt, and your feet feel like bricks. Plus, you're so hungry that your stomach stops growling and you just feel a hollow pit inside.

Over the next few days, you get weaker and weaker. Finally, you are unable to keep moving. Your family is forced to camp and forage for food in the woods, but you won't find enough to sustain you for much longer.

☞ **THE END**

I guess you and Ma agree about the fishing net," Pa says.

You smile and nod.

"I'll finish up the washing if you'll weave me the net," Pa offers Ma. Soon Ma has put together an impressive net.

"This should catch plenty of fish," Pa says, thanking her.

Pa heads toward the river, and you run up behind him. He places his hand around your shoulder, and you walk together to the banks of the river. You grab one side of the net from Pa and fling it into the water.

SPLASH! Your hand accidentally gets stuck in the net, and you fall into the water. You manage to get out of tangle and swim back to the banks with the net, where Pa gives you a hand and pulls you out.

"Let's try that again," Pa says, and you both have a good laugh about what happened.

You throw the net back into the water, and within a couple of hours, you are able to catch several fish for dinner. Ma whips up an amazing supper that leaves you satisfied. Even better, the fiddles come out for the first time in a long while, and everyone enjoys some music and dancing.

A few hours after you eat, you start feeling nauseated and are bent over with pain in your stomach. The night passes and you don't feel any better, spending most of it throwing up.

"I think I know what's wrong with you," Pa says as he sits with you through the night.

"What is it, Pa?" you ask, trying to sound brave.

"You must have swallowed some of the water from the lake, and it's making you sick," he replies. "You'll be fine."

But Pa is wrong. The next few days are very painful, and you don't get any better. You die of dysentery.

 THE END

You choose to ignore Archie's consistent growls and barks. You roll over and gently push him away, hoping to get a little more sleep. But thundering hoofbeats and angry shouts jolt you out of your sleep only a few short minutes later. Scrambling out of the tent, you're horrified to see a gang of bandits surrounding your wagon.

"Hand over all your money and valuables!" the masked leader growls. "Or else!"

Pa, Caleb, and the other families have no choice but to give them what they want. You are forced to give up the rest of your money and what few valuables you have left. The bandits disappear as

quickly as they arrived, leaving you and your family with nothing but the bare essentials in your wagon.

"They must've been watching us, waiting for us to go to sleep so they could strike," Pa says grimly. "No one heard anything?"

You realize with a sinking heart that Archie was trying to warn you about the bandits, but you decided to ignore his warning barks. Now you have no money left for when you get to Oregon. Starting a farm with nothing will be extremely challenging.

"What if we go back to Barlow's Gate and tell the toll operators?" you suggest. "Maybe they could help us catch the bandits."

Pa scratches his head. "That'll cost us days going back. But I suppose we don't have any other options, do we?"

You decide to make the trek back to the tollgate to hopefully get some assistance with the bandits. It's a tiring return journey, especially considering the steep incline of Laurel Hill you now have to climb back *up,* and the oxen grow slower and wearier by the hour. Your whole body aches as you finally make your way back to Barlow's Gate.

But when Pa tells your desperate situation to the toll operators, they are unsympathetic.

"Sorry, folks," one of the operators says, tipping his hat. "That's why you have to be especially careful around these parts. Bandits will snatch the shoes right off your feet if you're not keeping a sharp eye out. Not much we can do about it either."

You know you're never going to get your family's money back. Pa shakes his head, dejected.

You decide to build a small cabin at the base of the valley. Ma will sell pies and blankets to passing travelers, and Pa will hunt and sell furs and dried meat to those in need of supplies and food. It's a meager living, but it's still better than turning back. You can try to save up enough money to make your way to Oregon City next year.

☞ **THE END**

I think we should keep the wagon," you say.

"Me too," says Hannah. "I love the wagon."

"And I love all our food," Samuel adds.

Ma laughs. "I agree with the kids," she says. "We've come too far and carried our belongings for far too long to give them up now. And even though it's been slow going, we are still making progress."

"I think you're right," Pa says. "It would make me nervous to leave the wagon behind too."

You see the same relief you are feeling on the faces of Hannah and Samuel. The wagon has become your

traveling house away from home, and it feels wrong to give it up unless you absolutely have to.

Everyone else in your wagon train makes the same decision as your family. They agree that if you all work together, you can manage to clear the Trail and keep the wagons rolling, even if it is difficult. Besides, with all this practice, the team is getting faster at clearing away fallen trees. If it reaches a point where it becomes impossible, then you can consider abandoning the wagons. But not yet.

As you hike, you realize that even though the mountainous terrain is challenging, it is also beautiful. With all the tall trees, cliffs, canyons, and purple haze of snowcapped mountains in the distance, the views have been breathtaking.

As you're walking, the wind suddenly begins to blow and the temperature drops.

"That's a northern wind," Ma says, looking concerned.

"Look!" Samuel shouts. "It's snowing!"

Sure enough, flakes of snow fill the air. They land

on your arms and face. You open your mouth and feel the icy coldness melt on your tongue.

"It tastes sweet," you say, laughing. You haven't seen snow for so long, but it feels funny to see it now, when it's still only September.

Archie runs back and forth and barks at the flakes. Hannah just twirls, letting her apron fill with the white fluff.

But within minutes, the light snowfall turns into a fierce storm. The driving winds and thick sheet of white snow are hard to move through. And the animals seem to be scared as the icy cold air pelts their skin. They push against their yokes and kick as if they want to run away.

"Halt the wagons!" Caleb orders.

You watch as everyone huddles together, discussing what to do.

"Do you think we should take cover and make camp," Caleb asks, shouting over the wind, "and wait for the storm to pass?"

"Look at the animals," Pa says. "They might freeze

if we leave them standing in the cold. We need to keep them moving."

"In this?" Ma argues. "We can barely make out where we are going. We can just cover the animals with blankets."

"But maybe if we keep moving, we'll make it out of the storm area," another woman adds.

Back and forth they argue. You don't know which sounds like the best option. Part of you wants to camp, and you hope that you and your friends will be allowed to play in the snow. But you wonder if the arguments for moving forward make sense too.

What does everyone decide?

If you decide to make camp, turn to page 197

If you decide to keep moving, turn to page 191

I think we can manage on our own," Pa says, looking confident. "The raft I'm going to build will be so solid, it'll be like a boat."

After two days of working, the raft is finally ready. As always, you're impressed by Pa's craftsmanship.

Finally, the time arrives to load up the raft. Pa sets it in the water and ties it to the banks with thick ropes. He leads the animals and the wagon onto it, and it stays steady. Then he takes Ma and Hannah by the hand and seats them in the wagon. You and Samuel join them. When everything seems secure, Pa jumps onto the raft and cuts the ropes. You're off!

Pa has big poles he's using to steer the raft. He gives you a second one to help him, since you are the eldest and because you are the strongest swimmer in the family. It makes you feel important to hold the pole and help Pa. And it's fun to be on the river, floating along.

You travel for about an hour with no problem until suddenly the rapids grow faster and the water gets choppier. Pa struggles to keep the raft steady as it lurches in the water, and you try to help. But your pole snaps in half as you plunge it into the water.

"Hold on!" Pa shouts as the raft starts to rock violently. You feel your breakfast start to come up into your throat as you hold on to the wagon for dear life. But once the raft capsizes, you aren't able to grab on to anything and are flailing in the freezing water. You try to swim for shore, but you don't see anything, and your body starts to give out, exhausted.

☞ **THE END**

I think I should stay with my family," you respond. "If that's okay."

"No problem. We'll see you on the other side," Joseph says with smile.

You help Pa and some of the other men pull the raft out of the water and carry it to the mouth of the rapids. The path to get there isn't very long, but it's really slippery and narrow. You make your way slowly behind the raft, but you find it hard to keep your footing. Suddenly you hear a muffled shout as Samuel clings to your leg. He is dangling off a steep cliff that sits on the edge of the path!

You extend your hand to pull him up, but in the process, you slip yourself. Your hands are grabbing for anything to hold on to, but the ground is so wet that you slide down the side of the mountain.

 **THE END**

I think we should try the South Alternate Route," you finally say. "It seems like it will be a good choice. And I don't want to cross that river again either."

Ma gives you a grateful smile.

"Okay, it's settled, then," Pa says. "I'll tell Caleb and see what everyone else has decided."

Pa comes back and lets you all know that the other families are going to join you on the route.

"They feel the same way about the river," he says with a smile. "And I can't say I blame anyone."

You set off toward the south and hike without any problems for the first two days. By the third day, it gets drier and dustier, and you are disgusted as you pass the rotting carcasses of a dead ox and horse. There are flies hovering around them, and you cover your mouth and nose with your shirt to block the stench.

"Will that happen to our animals?" a horrified Samuel asks you as you hurry past them.

"I don't know, Sam," you reply. You don't add what else you are thinking: that you don't know what happened to the people who were with those animals either.

The next day you see something that takes your breath away. Enormous mountains made out of sand are spread out in front of you.

"Whoa. What are those?" Hannah asks, pointing.

"Those are the Bruneau Dunes," Caleb says. "They are made entirely of sand."

"Are we going to have to go all the way around them?" Samuel grumbles. He's been in a bad mood for the past few days, and his face is flushed as he frowns.

"Yes, unless we decide to go through them," Caleb says. "We can try that, because it will save us a day's travel at least. But it will be a challenge."

You gaze up at the massive piles of sand as everyone votes on which way to go. When it is your family's turn, what do you choose?

If you choose to go around the dunes, turn to page 219

If you choose to go through the dunes, turn to page 186

You lean forward and stretch out your arm as much as you can toward Eliza.

"Grab my hand!" you shout.

"I can't!" Eliza says. "I'll fall."

"No, you won't," you promise. "I'll pull you up."

"I'm scared," Eliza says, her face red from the exertion of holding on.

"Just try," you say. "Come on, Eliza! Grab on!"

Eliza finally lets go and manages to grab your hand. You hold on tight and try to pull her up with all your strength. But it feels impossible.

"Come on," you groan, pulling harder. Only instead of Eliza coming any farther up, you are pulled down! You try to grab on to something with your feet to stop yourself from sliding over the side of the cliff. But the force of gravity is too strong, and the next thing you know, you are tumbling down the side of the cliff with Eliza behind you.

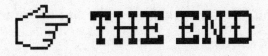 THE END

I think I need to get my shoes repaired again," you say, showing Ma how worn-out the bottoms have gotten. She gasps and covers her mouth in surprise.

"I'm so glad you said something!" she says. "How did your shoes wear out so quickly? The cobbler back at Fort Hall must not have done a good job."

"Yes," says Pa, shaking his head. "And we paid him good money, too. Your feet would have frozen while we traveled through these mountains."

Ma goes to look for some buckskin to repair your shoes. But soon she returns instead with the very same moccasin boots you had seen earlier, along with the wooden horse for Hannah and a miniature bow and arrow for Samuel.

"Try these on," Ma says, handing you the boots.

Slipping your foot inside, you're surprised by how light but sturdy they are.

"Are they comfortable?" Ma asks you, and you nod.

"Thank you," you say, thrilled to be out of your uncomfortable shoes.

You feel a mix of emotions on leaving the fort. The next time you will see civilization, it will be in Oregon City. And, as Caleb reminds you, you still have to walk more than 450 miles until you get there.

After a week and a half of hiking, your wagon train reaches what is known as Farewell Bend, where you will forever part ways with the Snake River.

"Even though it brought us challenges, I, for one, will be sorry to say goodbye to this river," Ma says. You wonder if she is thinking of the fresh fish or the water for the animals. It was hard enough crossing the river once; never mind multiple times.

"Are you feeling all right?" you ask, noticing that Ma looks a bit pale.

"I'm fine, dear," she says with a small smile. "My head is feeling a bit heavy is all."

You notice that Ma continues to look weaker over the next day, and she has to stop frequently because her stomach is unwell. At night, when you make camp, she asks you to take charge of making supper.

"I just need to lie down for a bit, and I'll be better," she says.

Pa builds a campfire, and you pull out the skillet and prepare beans flavored with bacon. You try to make Ma's cornbread, too, but it turns out like mush.

You notice Pa picking at his plate.

"I'm sorry the food isn't as good as Ma's," you say, a lump forming in your throat.

"No, no, it's delicious," Pa says, giving you a weak smile. "I'm just not feeling too hungry."

You hope Ma is better tomorrow, because nothing seems right with her sleeping at suppertime instead of being with the rest of you. But the next morning, she isn't better. And, even worse, Pa is sick too. Both your parents just lie in their tent instead of taking part in the usual morning routine.

"I'm sorry, kids," Pa says weakly from his feather mat. "We were both sick all night. We need to rest."

When it's time to roll the wagons, Caleb finds that your family isn't ready to leave yet.

"What's the matter?" he asks you with a frown.

You tell him about Ma and Pa, and he comes back with the man in your wagon train who is a vet. He has been serving as the doctor on your journey. The man goes into their tent and comes out looking grim.

"I'm afraid this is dysentery," he says. "Your parents need rest and plenty of fluids, and hopefully they will pull through."

The lump is back in your throat, and you swallow hard.

"What about the Trail?" you finally manage to ask, noticing how tiny your voice sounds.

Caleb gives you a sad look.

"I'm afraid I can't keep the rest of the wagon train waiting too long. I think I can convince everyone to camp for an extra day, though."

You just nod, grateful. Caleb gives you a pat on the back and hurries back to tell the rest. You spend the day trying to get your parents to eat or drink, but they can't manage to keep much down.

That evening, you peek into your parents' tent again.

"The wagon train is getting ready to roll out tomorrow," you say. "Are you going to be okay to go?"

"Do you think you can drive the oxen team?" Pa asks you. "We don't have the strength to walk, but Ma and I can ride in the wagon."

"But if you don't feel comfortable," Ma adds, "we can just wait until we are better to travel. We'll be able to move faster and can catch up with the rest of the train later."

You think about what both your parents say. As much as you like the idea of taking charge and leading the wagon yourself, it also makes you nervous. Already, it's been tough to be in charge and take care of everything on your own. Maybe a little more rest here, by the river, will be better for everyone. But you also hate the idea of being left behind.

What do you decide?

If you decide to steer the oxen and head out, turn to page 278

If you decide to stay camped a little longer, turn to page 179

kay, mister," you say reluctantly. "We don't have the money, but we have jewelry."

"I need to 'see it first," the man says as he coughs. "And we take half now, and the rest when we get to Oregon City."

You dig Ma's jewelry box out from the fabric-lined chest in the wagon that holds all your family's valuables and give it to Ma. The men take the jewels Ma offers them. You see one of them eyeing her wedding ring.

"This one I keep," she says firmly.

Even though you don't want to admit it, it's a relief to have the men's help. They help you pack up the wagon and cut wood for the campfire. You didn't realize how exhausted you were from doing your chores and Pa's, plus taking care of Ma.

But over the next couple of days, you start to feel weak, and by the third, you are riding in the wagon with Ma. You have caught a cold and soon you will follow Pa to his grave.

 **THE END**

That's okay, mister," you tell the man, standing as tall as you can. "I'm going to get my family to Oregon City on my own."

The men start to snicker softly, and you feel your face burn.

"Suit yourself," the leader finally says. "Good luck to you. And sorry for your loss."

Ma thanks them for their help, and they ride off. She tries to give you an encouraging nod and then goes to lie down in the wagon. You pack up the rest of your family's things with Samuel and Hannah and start the wagon rolling.

As you travel farther into the Blue Mountains, you try to hold on to the determined feeling that keeps you going. But as the days go by, Ma still isn't strong enough to walk. And you find the Trail almost impossible to navigate, with large trees blocking the path. You can't cut them up and move them on your own.

"What's that?" Samuel asks, pointing toward what looks like a little cottage nestled among the trees.

It's a small abandoned log cabin! You decide to stay in the cozy space for a while and give Ma time to heal. You learn how to set traps and hunt so you can feed your family through the long, cold winter. All the while, you think of Pa and what he would want you to do. That makes it easier. When spring comes around, you promise yourself, you'll find a way to continue on your journey somehow.

☞ THE END

I can steer the wagon so we don't fall behind," you say, trying to sound surer of yourself than you feel.

"I think that's a good decision," Pa says with a proud look on his face.

"I agree," Ma says. "It actually might not have been safe to stay here alone."

The next morning, you, Samuel, and Hannah break up your camp and pack up the wagon the best you can, with some help from the others. You lay Ma and Pa's feather mats in the back, after rearranging things to make it less lumpy.

Caleb helps Ma climb into the wagon and then turns to you.

"We're going to be approaching the Blue Mountains soon. It's good your family isn't staying behind," he says in a hushed voice. "I'd hate to think of what would happen to you if your parents took a turn for the worse."

You just nod. That was something you've been trying not to think about. Although this trip has been filled with challenges, you have never been as scared

as you are now. You've heard stories of orphans along
the Trail who have to either continue on their own
or depend on the generosity of others. It makes your
stomach turn, and you try to push the thought out of
your head.

"I'll send Joseph and Eliza to help you out
throughout the day," Caleb continues. "And if you
need anything, just shout."

You nod again and take a deep breath before
starting the oxen moving.

I have to push on, you tell yourself. *I have to get my
family to Oregon City.*

You've passed Farewell Bend now, and Snake
River is behind you. As your wagon train has to cut
its way through shoulder-tall sagebrush, the journey
is slow and exhausting. Up ahead are the famous
Blue Mountains, filled with woods and steep climbs.
You desperately hope Ma and Pa are better soon.
Hannah and Samuel are as helpful as they can be,
tending to Ma and Pa and listening to you without
arguing. You see both of them wipe back tears when
no one is looking, and you know how hard they are

trying to be brave, because you feel exactly the same way.

Over the next couple of days, you are relieved when Ma and Pa do start to improve. By the fourth day, Pa is walking next to you again, and Ma is sitting up in the wagon and smiling. You feel lighter, like a huge load has been lifted off your shoulders.

Look at those trees!" Samuel says, grinning widely as he runs up to you. "They must be more than two hundred feet tall!"

You've passed Flagstaff Hill and are now in the Blue Mountains. You stretch your neck upward to look at the massive fir trees around you. Like everyone, you've never seen anything like them before.

"I think you're right, Sam," you say, grabbing your brother and tickling him. "Let's see if you can climb to the top of one."

"You first!" Sam says, wiggling out of your reach and running away.

Archie seems amazed by the landscape too and runs ahead of you, sniffing at the ground and chasing birds. Even though it's only September, high up in the mountains, in the shade of the trees, the air has a chill to it. You look forward to making camp and sitting by the fire.

Ma fixes a nice supper, and you're glad to taste her cooking again. Even though no one complained when you were making supper, you know everyone else is happy too. When you are all done eating and talking about the day, someone pulls out a fiddle and starts singing. This kind of night is your favorite, as Samuel and Hannah start to dance and everyone claps. Finally, Ma puts out the fire, and you head to

bed. But as you lie on your feather mat, you can't fall asleep. You're thinking about all that has happened over the past week. Plus, you just can't get warm.

Archie is curled up in a ball next to Samuel, and you wish he were lying next to you instead. But then your brother would be cold. You pass Hannah, holding her doll tight and shivering underneath her blanket, as you head out of the tent to look for an extra blanket in the wagon.

Passing by the campsite, you notice an ember glowing faintly in the fire pit. You start to pick up a handful of dirt to smother it out, then pause. You wonder if you should add a few sticks to get a flame going and sit by it a bit longer to warm yourself up. Or should you just put it out and try to find another blanket and go back to bed?

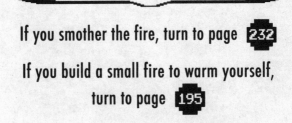

If you smother the fire, turn to page **232**

If you build a small fire to warm yourself,
turn to page **195**

I sure hope these ropes hold," Pa says.

You tighten the last rope from the tree to the side of the wagon. Pa carefully pushes the wagon to the edge. As the wagon makes its way down the steep incline, you hear the tree make a cracking sound. The weight of the wagon is making the tree bend forward.

Pa is looking down the side to make sure that the wagon stays straight and doesn't bang into the side of the mountain. You call out to him, but he doesn't respond. After several more attempts, he finally turns around and sees the tree. Almost immediately the tree snaps in half and goes whizzing by your face down the side of the mountain.

CRASH! You hear the loudest sound of your life. You walk over to the edge to look and see your wagon, smashed to bits and pieces. Your chances of making it Oregon have been crushed with it.

☞ **THE END**

You accept the Wasco people's offer to be canoed down the Columbia River. One of the men introduces himself as Tsuk as he shakes hands with Pa. They decide that Pa will take the wagon and the animals on the raft, while the rest of you will have Tsuk take you to the other side.

"It's better to be safe than sorry," Pa says. "Even though I know my raft would do the trick," he adds with a wink.

Ma and Samuel make it across the river first and are waiting for you and Hannah on the other side

when you step into the canoe, accepting the hand
Tsuk holds out for you. The ride is smooth and swift,
and as you approach the banks of the river, Pa is
already moving the wagon off the raft and speaking
to Caleb about how to get across the Cascade Rapids,
up ahead. You thank Tsuk for the canoe ride, then
huddle up by Caleb, who gathers everyone together
and tells you the plan.

"I will take all the animals around the south side
of the mountain and meet you on the other side of

the rapids. It's too dangerous for us to put everything on the raft and try to get across," Caleb says.

Everyone agrees. The wagons are lined up, and Caleb ties the final ropes to attach the animals together. Joseph and Eliza run over to you as some of the families make their way onto the rafts.

"Why don't you come with us?" Joseph says. "We could use another hand."

Do you ask Ma and Pa to go with them, or do you stick with your family?

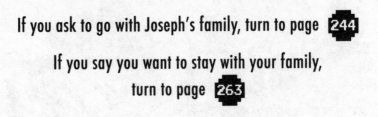

If you ask to go with Joseph's family, turn to page **244**

If you say you want to stay with your family,
turn to page **263**

You decide that while both options are risky, weighing the wagons down with heavy logs still sounds like a better option. The ropes might not be able to hold the weight of the heavy wagons and snap, which would be disastrous. Your family votes to cut down logs rather than attempt lowering the wagons.

"I agree," says Caleb. "I think the incline is too steep to try something like that here. That, and I don't know if we'd all have the strength to lower even one wagon. If one of us gives out, we're sunk. Let's stop for a while to catch our breath, then cut down a couple of these enormous trees to drag behind the wagons."

You're glad for the chance to rest, however short it may be. You, Joseph, and Eliza make a game out of picking out the tallest trees in sight and imagining how long it would take you to climb up to the top branches.

Pa, Caleb, and the others cut down several hefty trees and tie the logs up to the backs of the wagons. Still, it's going to be a treacherous descent, and the oxen are already tugging at their ropes.

Slowly but surely, the wagons descend the steep incline of Laurel Hill. The trek down is rocky, slipperier than you imagined, covered with moss and wet leaves, and more than a little frightening. But the trees dragging behind the wagons help to keep everything from careening down the hill. The oxen resist the steep incline initially, but eventually you and Pa help calm them down enough to carefully lead them down to the bottom.

Although your legs are hurting and tired from balancing your own trek down the slope, you can see the valley stretching out ahead. The landscape beyond is unlike anything you've ever seen—covered with lush grass meadows, mossy nooks, and thick pine trees rising into the distance. You think you see something misty obscuring the trees—maybe smoke from a nearby campfire, but you're moving too quickly, and you dismiss it as just a wisp of cloud.

"We did it!" you cheer as Archie barks in excitement. You, Joseph, and Eliza exchange relieved grins.

Caleb finally gives the order to camp for the night, and despite exhaustion, everyone's spirits are high. You and Joseph trap a few rabbits hiding among the trees. You bring them back to Ma, and she cooks up a hearty rabbit stew, along with the usual beans and pan bread. You're bone-weary but relieved that the worst of the mountain journey seems to be behind you. Oregon City is so close, you can almost see it through the thick trees.

But as you drift off to sleep, Archie's barking wakes you up. You groan and try to roll over, but then you feel teeth digging into your clothes. Archie tries to pull you off your bedroll and drag you outside the tent.

"Get off, Archie!" you grumble, wiggling away. "What's the matter with you?"

Archie bolts outside the tent, still barking wildly. When he pulls at your clothes again, you finally peer outside. Even with your bleary-eyed vision, you don't see anything out of the ordinary.

"Be quiet, Archie!" you order. "There's nothing out there!"

But he continues to bark.

With a groan, you eventually clamber out of your tent. Archie wouldn't just be barking like this for nothing. Maybe, just to be safe, you should ask someone on watch. You find the guard near one of the wagons, adding another log to the dying fire.

"I haven't seen anything," he says with a shrug. "Maybe your dog just smelled a skunk nearby."

"Maybe," you say doubtfully. Archie's ears are pricked, and his nose twitches. There could be a more dangerous animal around, but with someone on guard duty, you feel more at ease.

But Archie tugs on your clothes again and keeps barking. It looks like he's trying to lead you somewhere. But where? You hesitate. Should you see where he's trying to lead you?

If you follow Archie to see where he takes you, turn to page **319**

If you ignore him and try to sleep, turn to page **253**

You try your best to make your way over to the darker spot under the ice. Your clothes are feeling heavy and are weighing you down. The water is freezing, and with every stroke that you make to get closer to the darker spot, it feels like you have used all your energy. A little bubble of air escapes your mouth, and you know that you're running out of time.

The sound of voices is coming through the ice, and you can't really tell what is being said, but you know it must be Joseph and Samuel. Finally, you reach the spot of ice you were swimming toward. You try to push up against the ice and punch a hole in it. Another little bubble of air escapes your mouth. For a second, everything seems dark, and then you try pushing up on the ice again. But nothing is working!

Joseph's voice is getting louder, and you can make out what he is saying.

"Tap on the ice so I know where you are!" Joseph shouts.

With all your strength, you try to push up on the ice, but it just won't budge. You keep punching and pounding on the ice, but it remains solid as steel.

"Help!" you scream under the water, and all the air escapes your mouth.

Your arms are getting tired and you keep trying to kick with your legs, but you are sinking farther down, away from the ice. You reach out your arms, but you have sunk too far down.

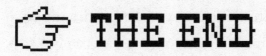 **THE END**

"I think it makes more sense to stick with the Trail," you say after thinking it over. "The dunes sound a little scary to me."

"What do you think?" Pa asks Ma and Hannah. "Can you handle more river crossings?"

"We'll have to," Ma says, while Hannah nods her head bravely. "It's more feasible than the dunes." She sighs. "It'll be good practice for the Columbia River, ahead."

"It's settled, then," Pa says. "I'll tell Caleb what we have decided."

The rest of the wagon train agrees with you,

except for a couple of folks, and they don't take much convincing. At this point, no one in the group wants to split up unless there is absolutely no other choice. There's safety in numbers, and as things get harder along the Trail, you have to work together as a team to survive.

The first time you cross Snake River again, you help Caleb and Pa tie the wagons together in order to float them across the river. The current is strong, and you worry you'll lose oxen in the water, but everyone makes it without a hitch.

After trekking aggressively for a day and a half, you reach the next Snake River crossing. Everyone decides to rest for a few hours before facing the river again.

★ ★ ★

It's time to rally!" says Pa as he grabs a tool to fasten the wagon wheels.

The cold water shocks the oxen, and they buck when they enter the water.

Caleb's face screws up with concern. "They're going to break an axle!" he shouts.

An ox breaks out of the yoke and floats adrift down the river. No one is able to swim fast enough to catch it. The axle is broken too.

You finally get everyone across the river, and you're thankful you didn't lose more than one ox as Pa replaces the broken axle.

You fall back into the routine of hiking for the next few days, heading north toward the Boise River, a tributary of the Snake River. The dusty trail is filled with sage bushes and not much else. Along the way, you spot more tombstones and simple grave markers of unlucky pioneers who have traveled before you but not made it. Some are proper gravestones etched with people's names, while others are just piles of rocks.

The graves that look like they have been there for a while have weeds growing around them. Others are fresher, more recently dug. You notice one covered with a thick layer of rocks to keep coyotes and other animals from digging up whoever lies there. It makes you shudder.

"'Here lies Bill. He didn't make it up the hill,'" Joseph says after seeing your expression, pretending to read from the gravestone of a man named William Smith.

"Is that really what it says?" Samuel asks, since he is still learning how to read.

"Yes," Joseph says, winking at you. You smile back. Your friend can always make jokes to lighten the mood.

After you've been hiking for several miles along the dusty trail, the mountains to your right and the rock bank to your left start to recede. A green valley suddenly comes into view.

"This is Bonneville Point," Caleb says with a flourish of his hand. "And that is the Boise River Valley."

Everyone is thrilled to see green grass for the first time in so long.

"Look at the trees," Ma says, pointing toward them with a smile. "This is nice."

The next day, as you enter into the valley, Caleb halts the wagons early for your midday break and gives you some extra time to rest.

"Can we go play for a little while?" you ask Ma as she prepares a snack for the family with leftovers from breakfast.

"Yes," she agrees. "But don't go too far, and don't delay coming back."

"Let's race over there!" Eliza points toward a few trees in the distance, and suddenly your tired legs are reenergized. You dash off toward the trees, with Joseph close behind you.

"I'm going to beat you all to the top," Eliza challenges, starting to climb a tree. You are always impressed with Eliza's ability to run, jump, and climb. Before you know it, she is halfway up the tree, and you start to climb after her.

As you reach into the branches to get higher, you hear a buzzing sound. Alarmed, you look around, but it's just some honeybees. Then you notice a beehive hanging from a branch above you, and your heart starts to beat faster.

"*B-b-bees,*" you tell your friends in a hushed voice.

"Get down," Eliza says, quickly making her way down the tree. "You don't want to get stung."

"Wait! Let's smoke out the bees first and get the honey," Joseph says.

"What do you mean?" you ask, shrinking away from the hive.

"We'll get the bees to leave their nest, and cut out some of the honeycomb to eat," Joseph explains, getting excited.

"But isn't that dangerous?" you ask, eyeing the bees suspiciously.

"No," Joseph says. "I know what I'm doing, and I'll do it. And besides, can't you already taste the honey?"

You imagine delicious, sweet honey, dripping off the honeycomb. You haven't tasted anything new for weeks now, and it is tempting to think of spreading the honey on your leftover cornbread from this morning. But you're a little nervous about getting stung by a bee, which has never happened to you before. Plus, Ma told you not to be gone for too long.

What do you say to Joseph?

If you agree to collect the honey, turn to page 202

If you tell Joseph you want to go back, turn to page 239

You think about everything until your head starts
to hurt, and you still don't know what to do. Then
you look over at Ma and your siblings. It looks like
they are broken, and you feel the same on the inside.
You can't imagine them pushing on any farther on the
Trail, at least not right now. Ma is still so weak, and
now with Pa gone, you worry if she will continue to
get better, or . . . you can't even think about it.

Samuel helps you dig a grave for Pa. He puts on
his bravest face and cries as he works the ground. You
think about how the shovel you are using was meant
for the new farm your family was supposed to have in
Oregon, and your tears fall onto the dirt. But you dig
the deepest grave you can so no animals can get to
Pa's body. And then you cover the dirt mound with as
many rocks as you can find. Finally, you scratch Pa's
initials and the date onto a big flat rock and use it as
a tombstone.

Ma watches you and Samuel work and holds tight
to Hannah. When you tell her your decision to go
back to Fort Boise, she just nods absently, staring at

Pa's grave. You follow her eyes and wonder if you are thinking the same thing. *Will I ever come back here to visit Pa again?*

As you leave the campsite, heaviness settles over your heart, and your throat tightens up. You scatter a handful of wildflowers over Pa's grave and then don't turn around again. You're not sure how you manage, but soon you lead your family back to the fort. There you find a kind fur trader who says you are welcome to make camp and stay for as long as you need. Over the next month, he gives you small jobs, helping outfit pioneers who pass through for the mountains.

You resole shoes, sell Ma's quilts and pies, and help find guides for those who need them.

As time goes by and you hear the stories and dreams of other families, you realize that you don't want to go back to Kentucky. The Trail is a part of your life now, and it's the dream Pa wanted for you. Even if it wasn't meant to happen now, you'll try again to get to Oregon City next year.

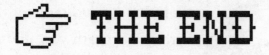 THE END

That sounds sweet," Pa says with a grin as you tell Ma she should get the goodies for the family.

Ma comes back with jars of sweet molasses and a sack of sugar. Your family leaves the fort in a good mood and continues up the side of the mountains. Like everyone else, you start off feeling refreshed, but after a few days, you have trouble keeping up. It seems with every step you take, you feel more and more of the ground beneath you, and it hurts.

"Is everything okay?" Joseph falls back and asks you.

"My feet are killing me," you respond. You lift up your shoe to show Joseph.

"I can almost see through to your socks!" Joseph cries. "Why didn't you get your shoes fixed when we stopped?"

You hang your head. "I know. I should've told Ma that I needed new shoes when we were at Fort Boise."

"I have an extra pair of socks," Joseph offers. "Do you want to borrow them?" You thank Joseph but really don't want to wear his smelly socks. *I'll be okay,* you think.

A blanket of white snow is covering the ground ahead, and as you continue up the side of the mountain, the snow is getting deeper. At first you can feel the icy wetness seeping into your shoe, and it makes your sock damp and uncomfortable. But after some hours of walking, you don't even notice it anymore.

When you finally stop to make camp for the night, you sit for a moment and look down at your feet. Your toe is poking out from the front of one shoe, and you find it strange that you didn't even feel it. You untie your shoe and pull off your sock. Your toes are a strange shade of purple and green. *Yuck!* You've never seen anything like it.

You head over to the campfire that Ma has gotten started and sit down with your feet as close to the flames as possible. Ma isn't in sight, and you know she must have gone to gather dishes from the wagon.

You see the kettle for heating water on the fire and have a thought. Should you use some of the heated water to soak them for a little bit? Or should you just sit by the fire and rub your toes to get them back to their normal color?

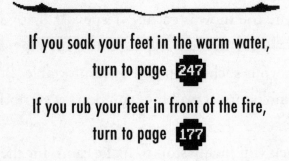

If you soak your feet in the warm water,
turn to page 247

If you rub your feet in front of the fire,
turn to page 177

"**H**annah!" you shout.
"Run! Bear!"

Hannah looks up, and horror fills her face. She lets go of her apron, and all the berries tumble onto the ground. And then, without turning around, she starts to run toward you.

You race back to camp, with Samuel two paces ahead of you both. Even though you want to look behind you to make sure the bear isn't following you, you don't. Instead, you just keep running.

Suddenly your foot strikes a big rock in the ground. It sends you flying in the air, and you land hard on the back of your head and are knocked out.

The next thing you know, you are lying on your back, inside your tent. Ma is leaning over you.

"You hit your head," she says, wiping her eyes. "How are you feeling now?"

"I'm okay," you start to say, trying to sit up. But

you are struck with a wave of dizziness and feel like you are going to vomit.

"Lie back down," Ma says.

You fall asleep and don't wake for a long time. Someone tries to shake you, but you can't bring yourself to open your eyes. When you finally do, you see someone but can't recognize who it is.

"Who are you?" you ask. "What am I doing here?"

"I'm your mother," the woman answers. "How are you feeling, my dear?"

You stare at the woman speaking to you but still don't recognize her.

"Where am I?" you ask.

"We are on our way to Oregon," the woman says, while a man rushes into the tent and starts to speak.

It's all making you terribly tired to listen to them trying to tell you who you are and what is happening. You close your eyes. And never open them again.

☞ THE END

You move toward the lighter spot in the ice, which means there is no snow on top of it. Carefully, you swim toward the spot, until you see sunlight. It's the hole! You stick out your head and take in a deep breath of air, trying not to gasp. The calmer you stay, the more likely you will get out alive. So you tread water for the next minute, trying to think about what to do.

"Help me!" you try to shout as you look around for anyone who can pull you out. But your voice is hoarse and comes out only as a whisper. Samuel is nowhere in sight. You are on your own.

You find the thickest piece of ice on the side to hold on to and slowly lift yourself halfway out of the water, leaning on your elbows. You're nervous you'll break the ice again and end up back in the water. Gently, you lean forward and kick your feet to help push yourself. You slowly make your way out, then lie on the ice and snow, panting, exhausted, and shivering.

Standing back up could mean falling through the

ice again, so instead you roll toward the edge of the pond. Finally, when you're sure it's safe, you get on your knees and stand up on firm ground. *Phew!*

You're numb from the cold but run back to camp. When you get there, Ma gasps when she sees you drenched and shivering. She grabs you and orders you to take off all your wet clothes. Then she brings you dry ones, wraps you in a blanket, and sits you in front of the fire.

"Thank goodness you got out of there," she cries, holding you tight and trying to warm you as you tell her and Pa what happened.

"You did everything right," Pa says. "That was extremely dangerous, and you could have been trapped . . ."

Pa's voice gets choked up, and he can't finish his sentence. Instead, he just shakes his head as if he's pushing out the thought, gives you a quick hug, and fixes you a steaming mug of hot coffee to drink.

Your family is back on the Trail the

next morning. It was a close call, but for now it seems like you escaped your fall into the icy pond without getting hurt or sick.

The next several days are uneventful as you make your way through the mountains. Everyone is getting increasingly excited as the end of your journey is becoming more of a reality. You are only a few weeks away from Oregon City!

Your wagon train has finally reached an area known as The Dalles, which you've been hearing about for weeks. It's where the Columbia River sinks into an area filled with massive boulders. Up until a couple of years ago, all pioneers had to travel down the swift river rapids on rafts they built themselves. But ever since a man named Samuel Barlow built a new road to the south that goes around Mount Hood, there's another option too.

"This might be the biggest decision of our trip," Ma says, staring at the rushing rapids with you. "Do we travel down this or go around it?"

"Why wouldn't we just go around?" you ask.

"Well, the Barlow Road costs five dollars a wagon, and we don't have much money left," Ma explains. "And it has its own challenges, including a very steep hill."

Another steep hill! None of the others you've encountered on the Trail have been easy. And five dollars is a lot of money, which you'll need to start your farm. But the rapids look equally dangerous, like they could easily flip a raft. You hear everyone debating the pros and cons of each. Not everyone has enough money left for the toll. In the end, they agree that every family must choose the route that it feels most comfortable taking. What does yours decide?

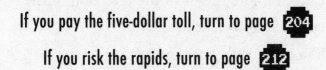

If you pay the five-dollar toll, turn to page **204**

If you risk the rapids, turn to page **212**

Shoo!" you shout, waving your arms around. The big cat continues to stare at you, muscles tensed, without blinking. You steel your nerves and fight the urge to run. Instead you pick up the biggest stone you can find. Flinging it in the direction of the lynx, you continue to yell at it.

"Go on, now!" you shout. "Go!"

Archie starts to bark at the lynx too. Together, the two of you make such a ruckus that the lynx finally turns its head and slinks away.

You breathe an enormous sigh of relief and realize you are drenched in sweat.

"Come on, Archie," you say, grabbing a few branches for the fire. You race back to camp and arrive breathless.

"I saw a lynx!" you shout to Joseph, the first person you see.

"How close was it?" he asks, his eyes wide.

"As close as you are to me," you say, realizing how close that really was, since Joseph is within arm's reach.

"Lynxes are usually awake at night," Joseph tells you. "It might have been roaming around in the early morning because it was hungry."

You feel the hair on your arms stand up. Good thing you scared it away.

After you hand Ma the firewood, she quickly fixes breakfast. Soon you are sinking your teeth into a stack of flapjacks and almost forget about the fact that maybe you could have been the morning meal of a big cat.

The wagon train starts rolling again a short while later. As you make your way higher into the Blue Mountains, the Trail has been getting harder to travel. Along the way, giant trees and branches lie in your path, making it difficult for the wagons to pass through. An hour after you start your day's hike today, another fallen tree blocks the way.

"Halt the wagons!" Caleb shouts. "We have to clear the path."

For the next two hours, the men of the wagon train work hard to chop up the tree and haul away the pieces. All the kids help by pulling large branches.

Everyone is exhausted by the time the work is done, but there's no time to rest. Caleb orders the wagons to start rolling again . . . until yet another tree needs to be cleared.

For the next several days, it's the same. The wagon train isn't covering much ground because you have to stop so frequently. Everyone is overtired, and tempers run short. It doesn't help that when the path is clear, the steep climbing is also slow and difficult. You, like everyone else, have blisters on the palms of your hands from dragging branches out of the way.

When Caleb finally halts the wagons for a midday rest, a man from the group starts to talk.

"We can keep moving at a snail's pace and

risk getting caught in more snow as we go up the mountains, or we can make a new plan," he says.

"Like what?" Pa asks.

"We could leave the wagons behind," he suggests. "We have only about two hundred and sixty miles to go before we're in Oregon City."

A few people snort and start to laugh. Leave the wagons behind! Ridiculous!

"Let's hear him out," Caleb says.

"If we just take what we need for the rest of the journey and tie it to the animals, we would move much more quickly," the man adds. "Plus, we have to think about how long our food supply will last if our trip lasts longer than expected."

Now some people murmur in agreement.

"Just think about it, everyone," Caleb says. "But for now, we have to keep moving."

You listen to Ma and Pa talk about what the man said.

"How could we possibly give up the wagon now?" Ma says. "We'd lose so much."

"Yes, but we do have to think about getting stuck

in the mountains in the colder weeks ahead if we keep moving so slowly," Pa says.

"But what if it gets better soon?" you ask.

"That's possible," Pa says, looking at each member of your family. "What do you think should we do?"

If you say you should abandon the wagon,
turn to page **184**

If you say you should keep the wagon,
turn to page **256**

You decide to see why Archie's so riled up and follow him. He continues to tug on your clothing and bark hysterically as he bounds away to the edge of camp. He leads you through the dark woods, whining, until finally, you smell something—it's not a skunk. It's smoke. Then, a glimmer of firelight just up ahead reveals that you and your wagon corral are not alone.

"*A campfire!*" you whisper, and grab Archie's collar, yanking him back. "Stay back, boy!" You

realize it's the smoke you saw through the trees earlier. But you don't know if these people are friendly.

Carefully, you edge closer to see who the strangers are. Against the firelight, you see several dark shapes, and you hear low voices. Your heart pounds as you overhear their conversation: they're gloating about all the unsuspecting wagon trains they've robbed on their final stretches to Oregon City. And, what's more, the bandits are talking about robbing *your* wagon train—tonight!

"Bandits, Archie!" you hiss. "Good job, boy!"

Together you slip away and rush back to camp, where you wake up Pa to warn him of the immediate danger.

"Good job," he tells you. "We could've lost everything." He hurries to wake Caleb, and they decide to tie up the bandits and bring them back with you to Oregon City so they can't continue to rob other unwitting travelers.

Pa orders you to stay with the wagons while they rush off to stop the bandits before they make their

Caleb and
deliver the ban

"We've bee
months," the sl
"They've been
Oregon Trail.
and vulnerable
so that's when

"They almo
for Archie! He

Archie tilts
curiously. The

"You don't
hero!" He digs
of jerky for Ar

Eventually
wagon families
Joseph, and El
again.

Thanks to
left over, Pa is
your own farm

own sneak attack on your wagon train. Ma, Hannah, and Samuel are awake from all the commotion and are shocked at the events.

"I'm just glad you're safe," Ma says, hugging you tightly. "They could've seen you!"

Eliza and Joseph join your family near the campfire.

"I can't believe we were almost robbed in the middle of the night!" Joseph says.

"It was Archie," you tell him. "If I hadn't followed him, we never would have been warned in time."

Eliza leans down to scratch Archie's ears. "You saved us, boy!" she croons. "You're such a good dog. A hero!"

Archie licks her hand and barks in return.

Pa and Caleb return within the next couple of hours with three disgruntled bandits—all tied up together. It would be a funny sight if they still didn't look so menacing.

"What should we do with them?" Caleb asks.

"Tie them to the back of one of the wagons,"

says Pa. "The
Oregon City
once we get t

The band
to follow you

"They're
wagons earlie

You can't
Archie boun
bandits, ensu

Even tho
has been esp
in your step
miles of woo
and Samuel
first. You can
chocolate cak

When yo
hardly believ
many buildin
hundreds of
start for your

him build your very own cabin, and it's even bigger than your house back in Kentucky!

The first night in your cabin is the best you can ever remember. Ma piles steak, corn, and potatoes with fresh beans onto your plate. And as a special surprise, she makes a rich chocolate cake for dessert. You may even sneak another slice!

Everything has ended up just as you had hoped. It's been a long, hard few months on the Oregon Trail, but it's been worth the journey. Oregon City is everything you've imagined it would be and more. You've successfully completed your incredible journey West!

☞ **THE END**

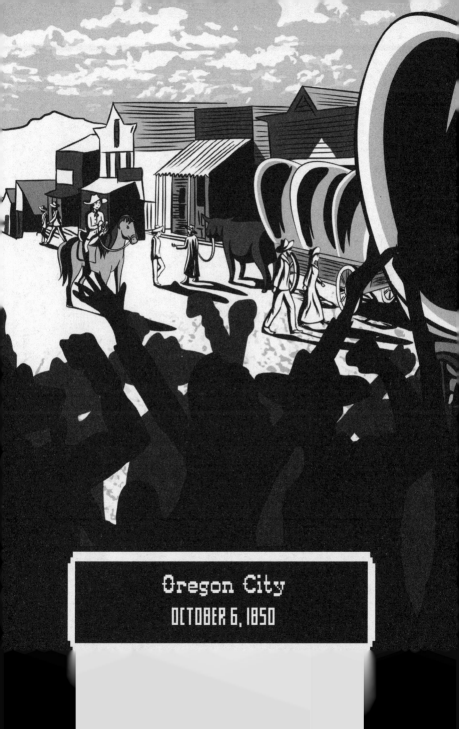

Oregon City

OCTOBER 6, 1850

GUIDE
to the Trail

THE FINAL STRETCH!

Congratulations on making it from Independence, Missouri, past Chimney Rock and through Devil's Gate all the way to Three Island Crossing, in what is now Idaho, on the Oregon Trail!

As you've already discovered in your travels across the prairie and desert terrain, surviving the journey of a lifetime requires you to be cautious and aware of your surroundings and to make smart decisions.

There's no substitute for being well prepared, so make sure to get all the information you need about what you will be facing ahead of time. This guide includes important facts about how to stay safe on the final leg of your trip across the Rocky Mountains to your destination, Oregon City! Read up, and get rolling on the Trail!

DANGERS!

CROSSING RIVERS

Crossing rivers can be necessary but always presents great risk. If you are unfamiliar with the river, you can quickly lose control of your raft to river rapids, which will dash your raft against the rocks. If you fall in, hypothermia likely isn't too far behind—the water is sure to be very cold. If you can, try to find someone more familiar with the river's navigation to help you across.

SAFETY IN NUMBERS

While it may be tempting to split up for various reasons, sticking together is better than going off alone in almost every situation. People in pioneer days didn't have ways to quickly communicate long-distance with one another, and if something happens to one part of the split-up group, the other won't have any way of knowing until it's too late.

RUGGED TERRAIN

Trekking through the mountains is treacherous and slow going. Look for roads and paths people have built before you, and be wary of cliffs and inclines, where it may be too steep to lower your wagons with ropes. You may need to weigh down the wagons to slow their descent.

FIRE

Stamp out campfires completely after use. If you become cold throughout the night, try to find extra blankets and layers, as it is dangerous to fall asleep in front of a campfire. You could catch fire before you even wake up.

DISEASE

Cholera and dysentery are common on the Trail. Many travelers died from contaminated food and water, so be sure your food is cooked and clean, and your water fully boiled. Rabies is also a danger in wild animals, and they can pass it on to your animals, who can pass it on to you. Do not touch wild animals or your own if they've been bitten. In the colder temperatures, frostbite and gangrene can be common if you don't have enough layers, which can result in loss of limbs and even death. Be sure to have thick, sturdy walking shoes so you don't lose your toes!

WEATHER

Be prepared to travel through a vast range of weather systems, ranging from bone-chilling snowstorms to bristling hot desert days. Even in the warmer months, sudden snowstorms still occur in higher rocky areas. Be sure to stick together and keep as many supplies as you can. Avalanches can also occur in higher elevations where there are fewer trees, so stay where the foliage is thick. If you fall into an icy lake and are trapped under the ice, be sure to look for spots that are lighter—this means there is no snow covering the ice, and it may be the hole through which you fell. In hotter, desert-like conditions, be wary of extreme fatigue, your wagon getting stuck in sand dunes, and lack of water leading to dehydration and death for you and your animals. If possible, avoid areas like this altogether, as you likely won't get far.

WILDLIFE

Watch out for bears, wildcats, and even honeybees. Bears and wild mountain cats such as lynxes may attack both animals and people. Although you may be running short on supplies, stay away from bees' nests, as bees are prone to sting if threatened.

DISHONEST PEOPLE

Sometimes people take advantage of others on the Trail, so be wary of passing traders. Bandits are infamous for attacking unsuspecting wagon trains at night. Stay on your guard.

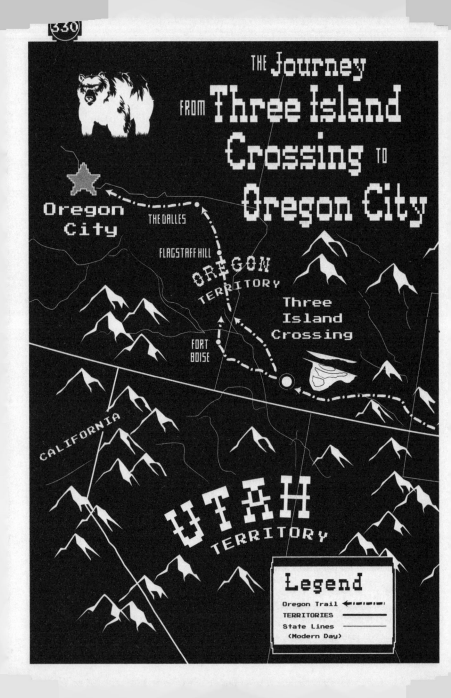

☞ FINDING YOUR WAY

In 1850, there aren't roads or many signs, and the maps are not very precise, particularly as you make your way into the mountains. There aren't even states yet. You have to navigate by using a compass and by keeping a sharp eye out for famous landmarks. The Trail is difficult to follow, particularly as you make your way into the mountains. Never leave the Trail or your group, and don't take shortcuts. Weather can be unpredictable in the mountains—keep a sharp eye at all times if you want to reach Oregon!

Look for these landmarks between and near Three Island Crossing and Oregon City

DISTANCE FROM INDEPENDENCE, MISSOURI:

FORT BOISE: 1,426 miles (2,295 km)

FLAGSTAFF HILL: 1,535 miles (2,470 km)

THE DALLES: 1,732 miles (2,787 km)

The Oregon Trail™

CONTINUE the Adventure!

Do you have what it takes to make it all the way to Oregon City?

Look straight into the face of danger and dysentery.

Read all four books in this new choose-your-own-trail series!